Title: Wildoak

Author: C. C. Harrington

Illustrator: Diana Sudyka

On-Sale Date: September 20, 2022

Format: Jacketed Hardcover

ISBN: 978-1-338-80386-0 || Price: $17.99 US

Ages: 8–12

Grades: 3–7

LOC Number: 2021044127

Length: 336 pages

Trim: 5-1/2 x 8-1/4 inches

Classification: General (F)

Animals / Lions, Tigers, Leopards, etc. (F)

Science & Nature / General (F)

--------------- *Additional Formats Available* -------------

Ebook ISBN: 978-1-338-80388-4

---------------------------------------------------------------

**Scholastic Press**
An Imprint of Scholastic Inc.
557 Broadway, New York, NY 10012
For information, contact us at:
tradepublicity@scholastic.com

# *WILDOAK* ADVANCE PRAISE

"In Maggie, C. C. Harrington has created a nuanced and complex protagonist. It is rare to encounter a character whose stutter is not portrayed as an obstacle to be overcome, but is instead an important part of her that is embraced and celebrated. Maggie is a relatable heroine who we can empathize with and be inspired by as we follow her trajectory from a place of pain and heartache to one of self-realization and fierce independence. Through it all, she stutters. Her stutter is part of who she is, but it does not define or limit her. We need more characters like Maggie."

—**TARO ALEXANDER**, founder of
SAY: The Stuttering Association for the Young

"This tender and hopeful story, with a whisper of magical realism, reminds readers that everyone struggles with something. C. C. Harrington's prose is beautiful, and she writes with a deep affection for the natural world. *Wildoak* reads like a classic. I loved it."

—**PAM MUÑOZ RYAN**, author of
the bestsellers *Esperanza Rising* and the Newbery Honor book *Echo*

"This well-told story of a girl's stuttering journey leaps and purrs on the back of a beautiful snow leopard."

—**VINCE VAWTER**, author of
the Newbery Honor book *Paperboy*

"This immersive read crackles with gorgeous descriptions and heart-racing action. Maggie is a fierce and kindhearted protector of the natural world. Her own severe stutter is thoughtfully and realistically portrayed as one part of the story's larger exploration of what it means to find the courage to speak for those who cannot by first discovering your own self-worth. Readers will cheer as Maggie and Rumpus team up to patiently guide them into a world of bravery and belonging they will never forget!"

—**NANCY TANDON**, MA, CCC-SLP,
and author of *The Way I Say It*

"*Wildoak* is one of those novels that makes us believe the world may well be as mysterious and as lovely and as possible as we had hoped. Maybe we can speak to animals in ways we never anticipated, and maybe we can sense consciousness in places we had never imagined, and maybe deep hurts can be overcome—the hurts of war, of humiliation, of pride. The rambunctious and sometimes frightening and sometimes incredibly funny story of Maggie and Rumpus is a story of how we might connect more deeply and more humanly—and so it is a story of immense hope. Read it, and be enlarged!"

—**GARY D. SCHMIDT**, author of
*Just Like That* and the Newbery Honor book *The Wednesday Wars*

WILDOAK

# WILD

# OAK

C.C. HARRINGTON

DRAWINGS AND DECORATIONS
BY DIANA SUDYKA
TO COME IN FINAL BOOK

SCHOLASTIC PRESS NEW YORK

Library of Congress Cataloging-in-Publication Data available

ISBN 978-1-338-80386-0

10 9 8 7 6 5 4 3 2 1 22 23 24 25 26

Printed in the U.S.A. 128

First edition, September 2022

The text of this book was set in TK.

The title type and author name were hand-lettered by TK.

The jacket art was created with gouache watercolor by Diana Sudyka.

The book was printed and bound at LSC Communications.

Production was overseen by Melissa Schirmer.

Manufacturing was supervised by Irene Chan.

The book was designed by Marijka Kostiw and edited by Tracy Mack.

*To all children who stutter.*

*To all who speak for the animals*

*and all who speak for the trees.*

Only if we understand, can we care.
Only if we care, will we help.
Only if we help, shall all be saved.

—DR. JANE GOODALL, *40 Years at Gombe*

# Prologue

Wildoak Forest was whisper-still. Spiderwebs glistened in the half-light, dipped in frost. Soft white snowflakes drifted down without a sound. Badgers huddled deep in their setts. A tawny owl swooped between the black-and-white branches, quiet as a ghost. And deep beneath the layers of fresh white snow and rich brown earth, the ancient trees spoke to one another, through a tapestry of roots and veins no finer than a spool of gossamer thread.

Then something happened in the forest that had never happened there before and would never happen again.

A van drove slowly down the lane, headlights groping through the whirling snow. A man got out. His leather shoes skidded along the ice-packed lane. He peered at the silhouettes of the tall trees and nodded. "This will do," he said, his breath melting into wisps. Then he switched on a flashlight and opened up the back of the van.

He unlocked a cage.

A cage that had no business carrying what it carried.

FEBRUARY

1963

LONDON, ENGLAND

# Chapter 1

Maggie pressed the tip of one finger against the point of her pencil. It was keen and sharp. But was it sharp *enough*? Surely. Her stomach felt hollow and shaky inside. In fact everything felt shaky, even her legs. She rolled the yellow pencil between her thumb and forefinger. She flipped and twisted it, tapping one end against the surface of her desk. *It was the only way out.*

Hilary Muir was next. She started reading at the top of page thirty-two, second paragraph, fourth sentence in. Her voice was crisp and light. It flowed like music.

Maggie bit her lip. If she could just get through the first line without stuttering. Maybe the rest would follow and then she could put away the pencil.

No.

She would block. She was bound to. Some of the words would come out fine, and then, suddenly, they wouldn't. The air would catch, her head would jerk around, her mouth would lock open, she would blink repeatedly, and every single person in the room would stare.

And laugh.

She squeezed her eyes shut. Laughing mouths and pointing fingers crowded in. She couldn't bear it. And then everyone would *know,* and she would have to move schools. Again.

She opened her eyes and glanced around. The classroom windows were locked. The door was closed. Old radiators clinked along the bare cream walls. The air was hot and stuffy. Louisa Walker sat on her right, listening, reading, following along with her ruler. They had never really talked, but she had always seemed kind. Maybe this time would be different, Maggie thought desperately. Maybe Louisa wouldn't laugh. Or Nicola. Nicola Robinson was kind too. *Lots of people were kind.*

There was a pause, a shuffling of feet, the rustling of pages.

"Thank you, Hilary. Well read—beautiful in fact. Margaret Stephens, please start at the bottom of page thirty-four." Miss Bryant's voice sounded muffled and far away as it drifted across the classroom. "Margaret?" she repeated.

A stifled giggle. Somebody was laughing already, and she hadn't even opened her mouth. Maggie could feel the wool of her sweater, tight around her neck.

"Margaret Stephens, are you listening to me?"

She stared down at the page, at the printed words, curling, pointed, full of sharp edges, like a mouthful of fishhooks. Miss Bryant's question hung in the air. Everyone was staring now. Waiting for her to start. *It's the only way out.* Maggie's heart thudded against her rib cage. She gripped the pencil. She pulled it back. *Now.* She drove the keenly sharpened point deep

down

into

the

soft

palm

of

her

left

hand.

She let out a gasp of shocked pain. Tears scalded her cheeks. Unsteadily, she rose to her feet and held up her arm. The pencil protruded from Maggie's hand like a grotesque oversized splinter. She trembled. Beads of scarlet blood escaped from the wound and dropped to the floor.

"Oh my goodness! Margaret, what on earth just happened? Are you all right? Quickly! You're excused! Get yourself to Nurse Nora right away! Go!"

Maggie ran out of the classroom, ignoring the sweep of horrified and disgusted faces. Nobody was laughing now. She kept running, holding her own hand, footsteps echoing along the corridors of Southam Primary. But more than the pain, she felt a rush of relief.

Nurse Nora was a large, plump woman with small eyes, a navy-blue uniform, and starched white cap. She moved with a cumbersome gait from one side of the room to the other.

"Margaret Stephens. Again? What is it this time?"

Maggie looked down. She held out her hand without saying anything.

"Well, how on earth did *that* happen? Speak up, child!"

Maggie continued to look down. Her excuses for being sent out had been getting more and more extreme.

There was no point in trying to explain. Nurse Nora of all people would never understand.

"You've been in here six times in three weeks. It's not normal." Nurse Nora sighed deeply. "You're almost twelve years old, Margaret. You can't possibly be this clumsy all the time."

Silence.

Nurse Nora glared. Maggie swallowed hard. It really hurt now, the throbbing in her hand.

"So once again you've got nothing to say for yourself. What a surprise."

Maggie stared at the toes of her shoes. She had not polished them, and they were scuffed and worn-looking. Why couldn't people see that none of this was a choice? She didn't *choose* to stutter. It wasn't a question of trying harder or breathing more slowly or whatever. She stuttered and couldn't help it, no matter what she tried to do or not do. Sometimes the words came out fine, but mostly they didn't.

The room suddenly felt small and cramped. She glanced at the door.

"Sit down," said Nurse Nora, following her gaze and pointing at a stool. "You're not going anywhere."

Maggie watched her rummage through one of the cabinets and pull down a large bottle of iodine and a jar of cotton balls. She unscrewed the cap with a high-pitched squeak. The dark yellow liquid soaked into the soft white fluff like a filthy stain. "This is going to hurt," she said.

Maggie stared at her, at the smallness of her eyes and dabs of pale blue eye shadow. *You're a terrible nurse,* she thought. *You've never made me feel better about anything.* She longed to snatch her hand away and run out.

Nurse Nora took hold of Maggie's wrist and placed her fat fingers around the pencil. She tugged. There was a faint squelching, and the pencil came loose, releasing a gush of blood. Quickly, Nurse Nora pressed down hard with the soaked cotton ball, covering the open wound with iodine. Maggie stifled a scream as the sting raced up her arm, burning like fire.

"You know, I've always thought there was something wrong with you, ever since you got here, Margaret." Nurse Nora fluttered her pale blue eyelids, apparently deep in thought. "It's your voice, isn't it? You try to hide it. I've seen you in the playground, sitting by yourself, not talking to the other children, even when they come up to you. It's not normal, not right." She transferred the pressure onto Maggie's good hand.

Maggie felt a wave of nausea and thought she might be sick. "Well, they can treat people with frozen mouth nowadays." Nurse Nora carried on talking, the words shooting out of her like little lead pellets. Maggie tried not to listen, but the woman kept on. "There are places, you know, special hospitals, institutions for the disabled. There's one in east London, and it's very well respected." She reached for a metal tray containing several needles and a spool of dark green thread. "I'm going to tell your parents about it. Granville Place, I think it's called."

Maggie shuddered. She had heard of Granville. Tom Baker from St. Anne's had been sent there months ago, because of his limp. Maggie remembered his mother at the school gates, all pink-eyed and teary. Everyone had talked about it. One of his friends had been to see him and claimed that kids were being locked into cupboards for crying and strapped down to their beds. He'd said the "doctors" had sounded all caring and nice to the parents, but on the inside it was a nightmare, with children so hungry they had to eat grass and toothpaste to keep themselves from starving. Grass and toothpaste.

Nurse Nora cleared her throat. She tapped a needle on the side of a metal tray. It made a soft pinging sound. She held it up between her thumb and forefinger.

"It's not right," she went on, threading the needle. "For somebody like you, Margaret, to be put in a class with properly behaved children. It's disruptive. And this, well, this is quite simply the final straw."

Maggie turned her face away and looked out the window. She did not want to give Nurse Nora the satisfaction of seeing that her words hurt. Even more than the pain in her hand.

"Now then, don't move." Nurse Nora squeezed Maggie's fingers and lifted the needle. Maggie clenched her good fist. She had never had stitches before. She stared at the grimy raindrops as they broke and trickled down the glass. And once again, from somewhere deep inside her heart, she felt the howl of wanting to be exactly like everyone else: To speak without stuttering, to say whatever she wanted to say. To be understood. To be heard.

The needle went in.

# Chapter 2

The snow leopard cub scooted his backside into the corner of the pen, reversing slowly, sinking lower and lower. His paws were still large and clumsy compared to the rest of his body, and he had yet to master the art of stealth. His long, fluffy tail flicked from side to side. His ears flattened. This was going to be an epic pounce. Back a little farther still, the length of his body winding up and up, a coiled spring in secret. Until—

Whoosh!

He sprang forward, leaping into the air, a rocket of fur, ready to knock his sister off the top of the ramp . . . but he missed . . . and came tumbling down on the other side of the pen in a heap of flailing limbs, too gawky to be graceful. His head hit the side of the ramp with a loud *thwump* and he rolled over, paws still swiping the air.

The female cub pranced sideways and scaled one of the climbing poles, delighted by her narrow escape. She was lean and agile, and her body moved like a ripple of silver-dappled water. She looked down on her brother, a glimmer of satisfaction in her bright blue eyes.

The male cub got back on his feet.

His tail was so long and furry, it looked as though he was being permanently electrocuted.

Tap-tap-tap.

The cubs turned to face an array of human faces, noses and fingers poking through the wired front of their pen. Eyes, staring. They all had predator eyes, set apart on the front, not to the side like prey. The male cub sniffed the air and gazed back for a moment. Then he turned and raced after his sister, his claws sinking deep into the stringy surface of the climbing pole. She darted even higher. But there was not enough space at the top for the two of them, and she swiftly batted him back down.

The humans tittered and pointed.

A woman wearing a brightly colored headscarf leaned closer toward the mesh. She tapped her fingernails against the taut wire some more.

Tap-tap-tap.

"What a cute baby leopard. Or is it a panther? What is it, darling? Oh, it's so sweet."

"I've no idea. It's got spots, probably a cheetah," said the man beside her.

"No, it's silver! Cheetahs are yellow. Oh, do look, here, kitty, kitty!"

Tap-tap-tappety-tap.

They continued to stare. The man had a long, thin nose that was pink at the tip. He sniffed up a drip of leaky mucus and pulled out his handkerchief.

"It must be a leopard," said the woman. "Do you think your sister would like a leopard? She has all those leopard-skin coats. What do you think?"

"Don't be daft, dear. Her flat is tiny." The man blew his nose.

"Darling, we're running out of ideas and time! Thirty is a big birthday. We need to find something . . . dramatic. Before tomorrow. Besides, her friend Violet, what's-her-name, that woman in Knightsbridge she always has tea with? She's got a pet lioness, and her place isn't much bigger."

"Oh, come on, dear. My sister can barely look after herself, let alone a large cat." He blew his nose again with a loud trumpeting sound, folded the handkerchief, and placed it back in the pocket of his overcoat. "And what would she do with it once the thing grows up?"

"Well, what else are we going to give her? We've

been through every department in the whole of Harrods! This is the most luxurious department store in the world. Queen Elizabeth shops here, for goodness' sake. Where else do you want to go? Besides, Arabella is terribly lonely."

The man narrowed his eyes for a moment and leaned in. His nostrils flared. His cold was getting worse, and he was tired of shopping.

"Perhaps it would be just the thing," he muttered. "Yes, perhaps you're right, dear." He checked his watch and leaned away from the pen. "I've changed my mind. I think it's an excellent idea. Dear?"

But the woman had moved on, intrigued by the armadillos for sale in the pen next door. The man turned and waved at one of the assistants in a smart green uniform hovering nearby.

"Excuse me? Yes—you. Thanks. I would like to buy one of these—er . . . what is it exactly?"

"A snow leopard, sir," said the man, dusting off one of his jacket lapels. *"Panthera uncia."*

"Right, yes, whatever. I want one. Can I have it delivered tomorrow, by any chance, to a specific address?"

"I'll just have to check the delivery options, sir, but

I doubt it'll be a problem. Would you prefer the male or the female?"

"Doesn't matter."

"Very well, sir. Give me a moment. There are some questions you'll need to answer and a few instructions to read through. Won't take long. If you'd care to follow me, we'll get you sorted out in a jiffy."

"Very well. Er, does it, do they have names?"

"You're welcome to change the names upon purchase, sir." The assistant smiled. "But yes, for the moment they go by Rumpus and Rosie."

"Ah." The man nodded. "Rather silly names if you ask me."

The assistant nodded, perhaps a little curtly. "As I said, sir, you're welcome to change the names upon purchase, as you see fit. This way, please."

"Dear! Come along, we have to fill out some paperwork. Gloria dear! Come along!" the man called out to the woman in the bright headscarf. She looked up and hurried back to him.

A few hours later, Rumpus and Rosie were curled up beside each other. They had fallen asleep, oblivious to the thinning crowd of shoppers and the ending of the day. Rumpus was dreaming. His eyes were shut tight, paws trembling. Rosie was on her back, her soft creamy underbelly sprawled sideways and thick, fluffy tail wrapped around her back legs like a blanket. Her nose was pressed up against her brother's fur. This was how they always slept, warmed by each other, comforted by each other.

A sudden shaft of bright light flooded the pen, and both of them woke with a start.

Large hands in white gloves reached forward, and Rumpus felt himself picked up by the scruff of his neck.

He mewed, wriggled, and swiped. Then he felt a sharp needle puncture his left flank, and within minutes, everything went dark.

# Chapter 3

Maggie shut the door to her bedroom, gently. She threw down her satchel and kicked off her school shoes. She loved her room. The low ceiling sloped at odd angles, creating nooks and cubbyholes so that she had to duck whenever she climbed into bed. She loved the small crooked cupboard hidden in the far corner. More specifically, she loved the *feeling* she got every time she crawled inside the cupboard. It was the feeling of being whole.

She peeled off her wool socks, damp from the wet, snowy walk home. The floorboards were cold but familiar and reassuring beneath the soles of her feet as she crossed the room. She lifted the cupboard latch with her good hand.

"Hi, everyone," she said. The space was just big enough for her and lit with thin strips of natural light from the open rafters above. There was enough room to sit cross-legged but not quite enough to stand up all the way. The walls were rough and unfinished, and lined with a single, slightly wonky shelf of pinewood. Along the shelf stood a series of boxes, jars, and neat stacks of newspapers. A small chopping board and knife rested at one end, covered in bits of carrot and sliced raisins.

"Wellington? Wellington, I'm back," she whispered, lifting a shoebox off the shelf and into her lap. The sides of the box had been cut open to make miniature windows and a front door that never closed.

"Hello, my friend," she said, nudging a nest of straw and bits of torn-up newspaper. A small brown mouse poked his head out, whiskers twitching. "How are you doing? I've got so much to tell you." Maggie paused. "It's not really a good kind of tell you. More of a bad kind of tell you." The mouse shook his head and dislodged little pieces of straw from behind his ears. Then he stood up on his hind legs and cocked his head to one side, almost as if he were listening.

It had been this way since Maggie could remember. Since the day her parents had first taken her to London Zoo and she'd seen the tiger. He had come up to her on the other side of the bars, close. Close enough for Maggie to look directly into his gold-amber eyes. "You're trying to tell me things," she had whispered, her small human heart beating hard. "But you can't get the words out, can you?"

Then, without thinking, she had started talking to the big cat and her words had flowed. No stuttering, no blocks, nothing. Mr. and Mrs. Stephens had stared, astonished by what was happening. Nobody had ever been able to understand the why or the how of it, but from that moment on, Maggie had not stuttered whenever she spoke to animals. She still didn't.

The mouse blinked. He washed his face, then scampered into Maggie's lap. "Looks like you've had a good nap," she said, stroking his smooth brown back with one finger. His tiny body was warm and soft. She picked him up. "Don't be worried," she said, raising her bandaged hand. "I'll tell you everything in just a minute. But let's do the rounds first. I want to say a proper hello to everybody. I missed you so much today, Wellington. I always miss you when I'm at school, but I especially missed you today."

Maggie let him sit out while she reached farther along the shelf. Then she picked up a small jam jar with a silver lid. The lid had been roughly pierced with a knife. It made a soft scraping sound as she unscrewed it. Two garden snails were stuck to the glass on the inside. One was nibbling a piece of not-very-crunchy-anymore cucumber.

"Hello, Spitfire, Hurricane. What's happening with you two? Looks like you could use a little more moisture," she said, making a mental note to add a thimbleful of water to their jar. "It's still too cold to let you back outside, but it won't be much longer. At least I hope not." The snails were calm and gentle. They moved slowly, their tentacle eyes taking in everything, not judging, not demanding, just a wondrous probing of the air. Maggie admired their shells, the swirls of rich browns, shimmering with different shades of light-speckled caramel and dark-flecked umber, twisted together in perfect symmetry.

She returned the lid and shuffled herself sideways, lifting up one side of a dusty brick. "And what about you four? Hi." Four roly-poly woodlice sprang into action, crawling all over the place and then, haphazardly, into the palm of her hand. Their little gray legs tickled as they ran about in zigzags, antennae waggling.

"Whoops! Ringo, no wait, George! Oh, Paul!" Two

of the roly-polies fell to the floor and immediately curled up into tiny, hard-shelled balls. "That probably didn't feel good . . ." Maggie picked them up gently, careful not to crush either of them between her fingertips. "I'm so sorry! This bandage is making me clumsy with all of you. I can't use my hands properly." She stopped, pushing aside the memory of Nurse Nora's stitching needle. "You're probably hungry," she whispered, shoveling all four of them back onto the old brick along with a few bits of chopped carrot. "There you go, try some of this."

Maggie scooted her body backward so that she could angle her head and look up toward the ceiling. A large brown spider was hanging serenely from a web beneath one of the eaves. "And how about you, Charlotte? How was your day?"

*Charlotte's Web* had been Maggie's favorite book for years, and it was obvious from the moment she had first found the spider fingering her way out of a bathroom sink what her name ought to be. But it was difficult trying to keep the roly-polies out of the wrong place at the wrong time, in a relatively small cupboard. Charlotte was a spider, after all.

Finally, Maggie turned and shuffled forward on

her knees so she could reach the other end of the crawl space. A large nook held a rickety wooden birdcage and the last of her pets, a wounded turtle dove. She slipped open the latch and put her good hand inside. The dove hopped onto her wrist, his claws gripping with a pointed, twig-like grasp. A few weeks ago, the bird had collided with the milkman's van and badly damaged one of his wings.

"And last but definitely not least. Hello, Flute. How's your wing feeling?" Maggie adjusted the dove's bandage. His dark orange eyes swiveled from side to side. "Look, I've got a bandage now too," she said. "We're twins!" She grinned. "Would you like to come out into my bedroom? Shall we go look out the window and see what we can see?"

BANG. BANG.

The door to the cupboard shook a little. Maggie stiffened.

"Sounds like Father is home," she said. With Flute still on her wrist, she edged backward and put her ear to the cupboard door. Her parents' voices could be heard rising through the floors below, loud and angry.

"When are you going to stop burying your head in the sand, Evelyn? For goodness' sake. She needs treatment!" Her father was shouting. "You heard the headmaster, you heard Nurse Nora! They don't want her. Full stop. We've tried three schools now. THREE in two years. There aren't any others. It's embarrassing. And I've had enough. I've had enough! Do you hear me? Margaret is going to Granville. It's what she needs."

Her mother's reply was quieter, her voice no more than a murmur and not quite loud enough for Maggie to hear. She strained her ears.

"That's nothing but gossip! Nobody beat Tom Baker for crying. Don't be ridiculous. Nurse Nora knows what she's talking about, she is a professional. It's time. And don't you start telling me what to do."

"Vince, please. Calm down! Just calm down!" Her mother's voice was raised now too. Maggie stayed absolutely still. "Please! Listen to me for a minute! Just one single minute. I've got an idea. I want you to really think about it." Her voice softened once again.

Flute ruffled his good wing. He held on to Maggie's wrist. "What'll happen to me now?" she whispered, stroking the bird. Her fingertips trembled. She stayed inside the cupboard for a long time, not moving until long after the voices below had blurred into muffled noise and she could no longer understand what either of her parents was saying.

# Chapter 4

The collar felt wrong. Very wrong. Rumpus sat back inside the crate and used his hind leg to try and scratch it off. Cuff-cuff-cuff-cuff-cuff. He couldn't. The collar went all the way around his neck, tight and uncomfortable. He extended his claws farther and tried again. Cuff-cuff-cuff-cuff-CUFF. The thing wouldn't shift. It was annoying. And jangly. The metal tags kept clinking under his chin.

The van jolted suddenly. Rumpus tumbled against the slatted walls of his crate and slid sideways. He was inside the back of a truck. Everything was in motion, bouncing him about. He wasn't sure where he was going. Or what had happened to his sister.

He put his nose in the air and sniffed. The smell of the exhaust was overpowering. He struggled to detect much else. Humans. Tarmac. Smog. There was plenty of noise, other engines, horns, wheels turning, traffic.

The truck started to slow. They turned a corner and then another. Rumpus skidded from one side to the next. He felt sick. The driver shifted gears, and the van slowed further until they eventually came to a stop. Rumpus could hear muffled voices, a door open and close, followed by the sound of footsteps sinking into soft snow and slush. Locks were unlocked, and flashes of early morning light fell through the slats of his crate. A blast of cold winter air. All of his senses tingled. He felt the crate sliding forward and gripped the wooden base to stop himself from tipping, his sharp claws puncturing the surface of the wood.

The two men eased the crate out of the truck, lowering it gently onto the icy pavement. Rumpus paced and circled inside. He pressed his face against the wooden bars so he could look out.

They were at one end of a long, wide street, lined with white buildings, smart steps, and columns with glossy front doors.

The driver of the truck rang one of the intercoms. It chimed like a bell. Rumpus kept circling.

"Ms. Arabella Pennyworth?"

"Yes?"

"Good morning. Special delivery for you, madam. From the Pet Kingdom, Harrods."

"Really?"

"Yes, madam."

"The Pet Kingdom? Harrods? Goodness. From whom exactly?"

Rumpus stopped pacing. His ears pricked forward. He could hear the ruffling of papers. And more voices.

"Er, from a Mr. and Mrs. Pennyworth. I believe it comes with birthday wishes, madam."

"Oh yes, that's my brother, Stanley, and his wife, Gloria! How lovely. I'll just get my coat and be right down."

Rumpus whipped around again. The crate was small. He wanted to get out. One of the drivers knelt down and peered in at him.

"All right there, little fellow. This is your new home, so it is. Good luck to you."

Rumpus could tell by the tone of the man's voice that he was trying to reassure him. It wasn't working. He pawed at the walls.

"Oi, stop that, she'll be here in a sec—"

Hinges swinging, a door opening. Ankles, high-heeled shoes clicking and sliding on the icy steps. Rumpus stopped and pressed his nose against the slats again. More voices. And then a pause.

A long pause.

"It's a what?"

"A snow leopard, madam."

Another pause.

"Gracious me. How on earth do I look after it?"

"If you could just sign here, madam, I'll get the papers for you, and we'll go through them together. There are plenty of helpful instructions."

"Very well. Oh, I say, how exotic!"

Rumpus could see three pairs of feet moving around. Shiny black shoes with dark green trouser legs and gold trim, glossy high heels, and a pair of old driver's boots. More voices, more rustling.

The woman got down on her knees, and a sliver of her face appeared. Her breath clouded the cold air. She smelled vaguely of . . . flowers? It was an unnatural, sickly smell. Rumpus couldn't help screwing his eyes shut and scrunching up his nose and whiskers. He sneezed.

"Look at you! Aren't you a pretty little thing? How amusing that my brother should give me a snow leopard during the biggest snow of the century!" Her eyes were rimmed with black, and her lashes were long and thick. She laughed. The sound was light and bubbly. Rumpus stared at her.

"Take it upstairs, gentlemen. Thank you."

Rumpus found the whole situation more and more confusing. And he was getting hungry. From what he could see, this new room was much bigger than the pen he had been in at the department store. But the woman still hadn't opened his crate. There had been a lot more talking and a very uncomfortable ride up several flights of stairs.

He scratched the sides of the crate impatiently, dragging his claws through the wood. It was past breakfast time. Clearly the woman who smelled of sickly flowers needed reminding of this Very Important Fact.

A telephone rang.

Rumpus tried biting the side of the crate.

It didn't make a difference. The woman was still not paying attention, and now she was talking some more.

"Hello? . . . Oh, Stanley . . . Yes, the leopard is here. It just arrived. Thank you! . . . Yes, I was totally surprised! . . . Oh, no, I'm delighted! What fun! No . . . I'm about to let him out. The man from Harrods was very helpful, not to worry. He showed me the box of food parcels, told me all about it, and yes . . . proper walks. He gave me a lead and everything . . . I've got the collar too, it's pretty, my favorite blue and so sparkly. I'm going to take him to the park shortly . . . Well, Mary is throwing a drinks party for me tonight, I can't . . . What? Oh, I'll just leave him in the cage thing . . . Oh yes, fine! It is terribly ugly though. Did they not sell kennel-type things? Something a bit less . . . rustic? . . . Oh, I see. All right, well, I can pop over next week. Yes, thank you again, Stanley. And tell Gloria I'm thrilled. Thank you . . . I do. I think we'll get on famously. He's so pretty-looking. Goodbye, Stanley."

Rumpus threw his shoulder against the back of the crate.

A moment later, the woman knelt down.

"Goodness, settle down. I shalln't let you out if you're going to be rough like that."

Rumpus could hear the sound of sliding bolts. He stood still, tail flicking from side to side.

The door swung open.

He padded out, cautiously.

It was a little bewildering. He had never been in a place with so much furniture or such large windows. Or felt carpet this soft and spongy. He couldn't help kneading it once or twice.

"Now, let's see. What's your name again. 'Rumpus'? Oh dear," said the woman, riffling through some of the papers the Harrods driver had given her. "I'm really not sure about that name. I'll have to think of a new one. Leopold, perhaps. Leopold the leopard? Yes, that sounds rather smart." She kept talking as she beckoned him toward the kitchen. "Come along, come over here into the kitchen. The delivery man has explained everything. I'm to give you something to eat now, and then we'll go for a walk."

Rumpus followed her warily, his long, fluffy tail swaying from side to side. He was overcome by a wave of intriguing new smells, but there was one in particular he could not ignore: raw meat.

The woman unwrapped a large parcel. "Oh gosh, these meatballs are rather . . . bloody." Rumpus paced impatiently back and forth beside the cabinets, the tips of his claws scrabbling against the tiles.

"All right, here you are." The woman placed a china plate on the floor, piled high with pinkish balls of ground-up beef. "Only the best for my new kitty." She leaned forward to stroke him but then changed her mind at the last minute and pulled back her hand.

Rumpus was so hungry he wolfed down the food in two short gulps. Then he licked his bright white teeth with his bright pink tongue. Instinctively, he looked around to see if Rosie had finished hers and whether or not he might be able to steal a few morsels. But then he remembered. She was not here. He called out for her, a soft mewling call.

"What are you looking for, Leopold? No, that still doesn't sound right." The woman cocked her head to one side. "You really need a proper name. How about Snowy, since it's so cold and you are a snow leopard after all? Do you want some more food, Snowy, is that why you're crying?" She bent forward to pick up the plate. "The driver said just four meatballs at a time. But I think three is enough. Come along, I'm going to take you for a walk. That'll cheer you up. Hyde Park is around the corner. And we can get a hot cocoa on the way back."

Rumpus looked at her, trying to understand.

# Chapter 5

Maggie sat by the coal fire in their small front room, still in her pajamas. Fragments of last night's argument echoed in her mind. She tried not to bite her nails. She didn't want to go back to Southam Primary, even if they'd have her. But Granville sounded terrifying.

"Evelyn!" shouted Mr. Stephens. "Come out of the kitchen, please. I'm waiting."

Maggie could tell he was annoyed. Annoyed and tired. He stood by the mantelpiece and adjusted the position of his tie even though it was straight to begin with. Vincent Stephens wore a tie every day, even at the weekends.

Mrs. Stephens hurried in, wiping her hands on her gingham apron. She came to sit on the narrow sofa, right beside Maggie. "Good morning, love," she whispered.

"Right. Your mother and I have been discussing your education," said Mr. Stephens.

Maggie took hold of her mother's hand and stared at her slippers. She held her breath.

"As you know, Mr. Boothe has informed us that you are no longer welcome at Southam Primary. Which means that—"

"N-n-n-n-n-no! You c-c-c-aaaaa-n't make me! I will not g-g-g—" Maggie burst out. *OH, PLEASE, please can the words just come out?* "I will not g-go to Gr-Gr-Gra—" She tried again. Her neck and shoulders started to jerk uncontrollably, back and forth, back and forth.

"Granville?" Her father finished off the word. "'Granville—that's what you're trying to say, isn't it?"

The block finally ended. Maggie stared at the bandage on her hand, at the large silver safety pin that kept it all together. She nodded softly.

"It's okay, love, you are not going to Granville," her mother said, giving her a gentle squeeze.

"We have decided that you are to spend a few weeks with your grandfather Fred Tremayne, in Cornwall," said Mr. Stephens.

Maggie looked up in shock. Grandpa Fred? She could hardly remember him. Mother talked to him on the phone, but she hadn't seen him for at least three or four years, ever since he and Father had had a terrible row. She wasn't sure why, something to do with the war maybe. Father's RAF medals lay polished in a small glass case on his desk, but he never talked about the war, ever.

"Your mother seems to think the countryside air will do you good," he said. "I think it's a long shot, to say the least." He started pacing around the small room. "But I'm prepared to give it a try on the following condition: If your stutter has not improved by the end of your stay, you will go to Granville Place for treatment."

"Vincent—" Mrs. Stephens stood up abruptly and faced him. "That is *not* what we agreed last night. What we agreed was that we would do further research while she's away, into other possible school options, but not Granville—"

"Don't start this again, Evelyn! The rumors about Granville are nothing but rumors. Tying children down . . . what rubbish. This is 1963, not 1923." Mr. Stephens wiped a drop of spittle from his chin.

"Fa-Fa-Fa-Fa-aaaaa-ather. Please. Mother. Stop. Stop. T-T-T." Maggie tried to get between them. She kept trying to speak, but the air wouldn't flow, her tongue wouldn't move, the words weren't coming out. She tried again. And again, and again.

"That's enough," said Mr. Stephens wearily. He put a firm hand on Maggie's shoulder, forcing her to sit back down. "I've made my decision. There is a train that leaves Paddington tomorrow. You may start packing." He straightened his tie again and walked out.

Maggie threw her arms around her mother and pressed her face into the warmth of her cardigan.

"All right, you're all right, my love," said Mrs. Stephens, holding her close.

Maggie didn't feel all right. She didn't even know Grandpa Fred, and she'd never been away for so long. Everything felt too sudden. She tried to take a deep breath in but found herself gasping.

"Hey, hey, look at me," said Mrs. Stephens, pulling back. "You're going to love Dad. He's a doctor. And he agrees a trip to the countryside could be really good for you."

"C_c_c_cuuuuuuuure me, you mean?" said Maggie, studying her mother's expression closely.

"No. *No.* Maggie, listen to me." She took hold of her face in her hands. "I love you. Do you understand me? I love everything about you. I love your gorgeous brown eyes and the way you see the world. I love your huge heart and how you care for all creatures, even the creepy crawly insects that nobody likes. I love your freckles and the chip on your front tooth and all the knobbly bits of you, your knees and elbows and the way your hair always comes loose, no matter how tight we tie it. And yes," she said, holding her gaze, "I love your voice too." She paused. "But right now, things are really hard for you. And that's what's bothering me. This is not about *curing* you. It's about finding another way forward."

"But F—-Father s-s-s-s-aid if I don't stop st-st-st-stuttering, I would have to g—g-g-g-g-o to that p-p-p-lace. I don't want to g—g-o there, Mother! Please . . . don't make me go."

"Give me time to work on Father. I know it's hard to understand, but I do believe, in his own way, he's trying to help."

Maggie wasn't sure she believed her, but she couldn't bear not to. Father would probably prefer it if she was locked away. He'd already made it clear that she embarrassed him. A child who didn't work properly, a broken one.

"Look at me, Maggie," urged Mrs. Stephens. She

squeezed her hand gently. "You're my girl. You can do this. And Cornwall is beautiful, lots of rolling hills, little stone villages, and hidden creeks. You don't remember it, I know, but I took you when you were little and you loved it. There are beaches too. The sea, love! Wait until you smell the air."

Maggie stared at her. She didn't remember it. All she knew was that it was a long way away, the farthest, western tip of England, and that Mother had been born there.

"Here, let's go upstairs and we'll do some packing together."

"Wh-what about my, my a-a—animals?" said Maggie, gripping her hand.

Mrs. Stephens hesitated. "Father feels strongly you ought to leave them here. But I'll feed them, I promise you."

"I can't! Ple-e-e-e-e—" Maggie's mouth froze open temporarily, and her neck jolted backward. *Not again.* In the corner of her eye, she could see her mother waiting patiently for the block to end. She was one of the few people who never looked away. "I c-c-an't be without them," said Maggie several seconds later. "I don't even know G-G-G-G-G-randpa Fred. And I've never been away from you."

"Maggie love, it was hard enough to get Father to agree to this in the first place. It will just be for a couple of weeks. Besides, your grandpa loves animals too, perhaps not quite as much as you, but almost. You'll make some new friends quickly, I'm sure of it." She got up and lightly smoothed out her apron, but her eyes were pleading.

Maggie wanted to be sick. She couldn't imagine not having her animals close by. She stared at her mother without even trying to say any of the things rocketing through her mind. The effort was too much. At moments like this, she wondered if she would always feel so lonely.

The next morning brought a fresh wave of snow. Maggie sat inside her cupboard, fully dressed in a pair of corduroys, thick blue sweater, coat, scarf, and red bobble hat. She had not slept well. Wellington nestled into the tassels of her scarf. She gave him a small piece of cheese to nibble on.

"Wellington, you know I'm not very good at saying how I feel," she said, stroking the top of his head.

"But perhaps you already know. This is hard for me, to leave you behind like this." She paused. "Please be extra good while I'm away. Mother doesn't really like mice, you know. You won't get any cuddles, but that's okay. Just don't cause any trouble." The mouse blinked, his small black eyes bright and shiny. He pricked his ears forward, and as always, it seemed to Maggie that he was listening carefully to everything she had to say.

"I'll come back for you. You know I will." Reluctantly, she scooped him up and laid him back inside the open shoebox. "Just please be extra good," she whispered. Then she turned and edged closer toward the nook at the other end of the cupboard. The mourning dove hopped from one foot to the other in anticipation of Maggie opening the cage. He cocked his head.

"Mother said you can stay in the kitchen while I'm gone, so she can keep a close eye on you," said Maggie. "It's a bit sunnier down there too." She touched his good wing, running her fingertips lightly along the silken metallic feathers. Flute looked her in the eye and bobbed his head, turring lightly. Maggie brought him onto her shoulder and let him sit there for a while. "You should be better in another week or two, maybe

Mum can release you then. Or maybe don't heal too quickly and wait for me to come back?" She swallowed hard. "I'd hate it if this was goodbye forever."

With Flute on her shoulder, she reached farther back along the shelf for the small silver jam jar. She held it up so the tip of her nose was almost touching the glass. "And you two take care of each other," she said to the snails. "Stay warm. When I come back, we'll be a bit closer to spring, I promise."

What she really wanted to say to all of them was just one word. *Goodbye.* But she couldn't bring herself to sound it out, so she stayed there, knees bent, watching the roly-polies trundle along the sideboard, with Flute on her shoulder and Wellington in her lap. "I'll miss all of you," she whispered, glancing up at Charlotte. "Each and every one of you."

She stayed with all of them until there was a gentle knocking on her bedroom door and her mother's voice telling her it was time.

Maggie was halfway downstairs when she stopped suddenly. "C-c-c-coming!" she shouted down. "One s-s-s-s——second . . ." Then she turned around and ran back into her room. "I just forgot one thing."

# Chapter 6

When Rumpus woke, the flat was dark and quiet. Moonlight fell through the kitchen windows, blending light and shadow into strange jagged shapes. He paced. The woman had not remembered to feed him, and he was hungry. He tried clawing at the door, certain it would not open.

It did.

It flipped wide open. She had not bolted it.

He crept out onto the plush carpet, the very tip of his tail flickering. He could see easily in the near darkness and slipped from one room into the next, searching for food. The kitchen smelled of citrus and some kind of cleaning fluid. Except the bin. The bin smelled much more interesting. It was tall, round, with a silver lid. Rumpus sensed traces of beef around the edge. Ears pricked, he tried to dislodge the lid by batting at the rim with his paw. It rocked from side to side. He tried with his other paw. Then he sat back on his haunches and batted with both paws interchangeably, like a boxer wearing furry, padded gloves. The bin wobbled from side to side and then toppled, spilling its contents all over the floor.

Rumpus jumped back, startled. He waited to make sure nothing inside would leap out and attack him. Then he edged forward, flaring his nostrils, cautiously pawing at the spread of scraps, wrappers, and all sorts of food containers lined with the remnants of everything from salmon mousse to a half-eaten Scotch egg. He sniffed tentatively, exploring this strange array of smells and tastes until he came across a crust of toast with Marmite on it. He stopped and screwed up his entire face into an exaggerated ball of repulsion. Lips curled, brow furrowed, and nose retracted, Rumpus began sneezing violently in an effort to get rid of the disgusting, tangy odor inside his nose and throat.

Moving on, he leapt up onto one of the countertops. But they were narrower than he expected, and he almost fell down again, his tail working hard to correct his balance. He discovered a half-open bottle of wine and a pot full of wooden spoons. The spoons made a racket when he knocked them to the floor and fell about like mysterious long-legged creatures trying to run away. He could not resist pouncing on all of them.

Caught mid-flip! The spoons scattered and clattered across the floor repeatedly. Rumpus was delighted and tossed them to and fro like a bunch of strange, long-legged creatures.

Once he tired of the spoons, he approached a large stand-alone shelving unit. The smells from there were also intriguing. He looked up. The unit was tall and narrow and filled with boxes, jars, dried foods, and baking supplies. From ground level, he wasn't sure if there was enough of a ledge to balance on, but he couldn't resist trying. So he leapt, the full length of his body springing upward in one fluid motion.

There was not enough of a ledge.

He slammed into the unit and bounced back off again, like a boomerang at high speed.

The collapse happened in a matter of seconds. Everything shook and came tumbling down in one tremendous, earsplitting crash. Rumpus skidded out of the way just in time. Glass shattered and wood splintered. He backed himself into a corner, crouching, until all the tinkling and splattering had died down and there was nothing but the silent sparkle of powdered sugar floating through the air.

But the smells!

He shook out his coat and padded over. The shelves lay broken on the floor, surrounded by chaos. A large green-and-gold tin teetered on its side. Then it slowly began to roll toward him, oozing a stream of thick golden syrup in its wake. Rumpus wasn't completely sure whether or not the tin was alive. He batted it softly. A dollop of sticky gold stuck to his paw. He sniffed it suspiciously and then licked it with the very tip of his tongue. The sweetness sizzled but did not disgust him. He licked a little more, then tried to clean his paw. But the syrup was very sticky. It stuck to his whiskers, his chin and, somehow, the tip of his tail too.

Feeling increasingly sick, Rumpus left the kitchen and went into the living room. His paws left large, sticky-powdery marks on the carpet. He looked around and caught sight of the heavy silk curtains. They looked a bit like bald tree trunks. Good for climbing. He sprang onto the nearest one, claws extended. But the shiny cloth ripped, and he slid back down. He tried several times until the cloth was fully shredded. Then he tried climbing other things instead, like the television cabinet and a large brass lamp. The lamp was not as sturdy as it seemed, and he was surprised by the sudden tipping and crashing of the thing. He leapt sideways and landed on the coffee table, but then his syrupy paws got stuck to a pile of magazines and he had to shake them off, tearing multiple pages in the process.

Rumpus was trying in vain to clean himself when he smelled something sickly sweet. Flowers but not flowers? The woman? He stopped and kept his body absolutely still, whiskers fanned, ears pricked. Footsteps. Human footsteps. The jangling of keys, the slide of a lock, the twist of a doorknob.

She was back.

# Chapter 7

Maggie could hear the doors slamming shut now, another whistle, then the slow chug of the train's engine. She kept waving until her mother was no longer in sight and Paddington station had slipped away. A moment later, she dipped her good hand into her pocket and drew out a small glass jar with a silver lid.

"I hope Mum doesn't mind too much," Maggie whispered to the two snails. "But I wasn't sure I could do this all on my own. And you won't cause any trouble, I know you won't." She eyed them carefully. "Spitfire, you're good in a crisis, and Hurricane, well, you're just good company all around, really." The snails appeared content as ever.

She placed the jar back in her pocket. Just knowing they were there helped to calm the shakiness inside her stomach. Although the lady in the seat opposite gave her a funny look. Maggie ignored her and hoped she wouldn't try to start a conversation. The thought of leaving home for so long was scary. At least, a few weeks away *felt* like a really long time, especially when she was used to staying in her room, or keeping to the back garden. Even so, as the train made its way out of London and into the snow-covered countryside, she couldn't help but feel a small prickle of excitement. She had never been farther than Shepherd's Bush by herself, and Cornwall was a lot, lot farther.

The light of day was fading by the time the train pulled into Truro station. Maggie stepped off, struggling with her suitcase. She lugged it over to an empty bench and immediately tried to figure out which person waiting around might be Grandpa Fred. None of them seemed likely, and nobody approached her. One by one, the platform emptied, and she found herself alone. She plumped up the bobble of her woolly red hat to make sure she could be easily seen, but there was nobody around to see her. Even the ticket office appeared to be deserted.

Maggie felt uneasy. She had not thought to ask her mother for Grandpa Fred's address. They had both assumed she wouldn't need it. For reassurance, she took off one mitten and slipped her hand back into her pocket. The glass jar felt smooth and cool to the touch. "I'm sure he'll come soon. Don't worry," she whispered.

Minutes added up. Dusk fell. Another train came and went. The circulation in Maggie's fingertips started to slow. She shivered. She was just considering whether or not she could face trying to speak to a stranger, asking what she should do, when she heard her name.

"Margaret Stephens! For sure it's you, there you are in the bright red hat! Forgive me, forgive me!"

She turned to see a tall man with pale blue eyes and thin white hair hurrying toward her. He was dressed in a tattered waxed jacket, thick wool scarf, and dirty Wellingtons. He smiled a soft-wrinkled smile that struck her as welcoming and a bit nervous at the same time. Something about his forehead, the set of his brow, reminded her of Mother. She couldn't help herself from smiling in return, mainly with relief.

"I got a flat tire! I'm so sorry! Of all the times to hit a blasted nail. Here, let me take that suitcase for you. You must be frozen. All right? How was the journey, Margaret? Or do you prefer Maggie?"

"F-f-f-f-f-f—" Block. Maggie pretended to cough. *Fine* was a simple word. The journey was *fine.* Why couldn't she just say it? Why couldn't the stuttering stop, for just a second, just this once?

She tried again. "F-f-f-f-f—" Then she tried switching the "f" for an "a." "All right, thanks," she said. "And I still p-p-p-p-refer M-M-M-M_________M." Block. "M___________." Why was Maggie always one of the hardest words in the world? It was a name, her name. But it was just a name. Her head jerked. "M_________." It was no use. Maggie waited for the block to pass, the seconds crawling into moments of eternity. *Maggie,* she wanted to say out loud. She preferred Maggie. When somebody called her Margaret, it made her feel like she'd done something wrong. It was what Father called her when he was angry. But instead she said, "I don't mind what you call me."

Grandpa Fred nodded, looking straight at her. "Right you are. Well, your mother still calls you Maggie, so we'll go with Maggie. And you can call me Fred. Everyone else does. I'm parked just over here. Mind your step."

She followed, picking her way through the snow and ice, grateful that at least he hadn't flinched.

Maggie sat in the front of a very old Land Rover. It smelled of damp, musty blankets, sodden earth, and . . .

mushrooms. In fact, she could see mushrooms of some kind, tiny white toadstools growing in between the seams of the hand brake. Clusters of green moss gathered inside the vent that didn't seem to be warming air of any kind. The only air she could feel was blasting through a gap in the rattling window, and it was freezing.

The Land Rover jerked and bounced along narrow, snowy roads. It became clear within minutes that Fred was a terrible driver. He kept looking over at her as he talked, which didn't help. They swerved multiple times and at one point almost hit a postbox. Maggie gripped the edge of her seat.

"So, Maggie, tell me," said Fred, shouting over the rumble of the engine. "What are you interested in? Your mother says you like animals?" Maggie nodded. "That's wonderful. So do I." Fred kept on talking. "What kind of animals do you like? Because I live in an old farmhouse, you know, although it's more of a cottage these days. There is an apple orchard and a family of robins nesting in the game larder. But don't go in there just yet. I hung a dead pheasant this morning, found him on the side of the road. Anyway, did Evelyn, your mother I mean, did she tell you about Cornwall at all?" He paused, just long enough to feel a silence settle. Then he started talking again, as if he wasn't sure whether the silence was a good thing or not. "Sometimes I wonder if I should've been the village vet rather than the village doctor," he continued. "Animals can be easier to understand if you know what I mean?" Then he paused, embarrassed. "I don't mean understand *you*, of course."

Maggie looked out the side window and pretended not to notice the awkwardness. She hoped he didn't mind her not talking.

"I collect acorns," said Fred, suddenly changing the subject and swerving around a blind corner. "And rocks. Shells and driftwood too whenever I can get down to the beaches. Have you ever seen a cowrie shell? They're hard to find. Tiny, beautiful little things, pale pink and white, no bigger than your fingernail."

Maggie listened. She gripped the sides of her seat a little harder, hoping desperately that nothing was coming the other way. Luckily the roads were unlike London roads, with hardly any traffic. He really was a terrible driver.

The sky was dark by the time they pulled into the small village of Rosemullion. Everything was wrapped in white. Maggie strained her eyes, not wanting to miss anything. They passed an old stone church with a pointed steeple, the village post office, a telephone box, and a pub with a red lion above the door. Everything was still in one piece; there were no big holes or piles of rubble like there were at the south end of Methley Street, where Nazi bombs had fallen and destroyed everything, leaving gaps like missing teeth. The houses here were not terraced or brick but separated out, each with a little gate and a small front garden, all coated in soft fresh snow. At the end of the village, the houses thinned out. The last thing they passed was a pair of huge rusted iron gates with chipped gold-tipped spikes.

"That's the old manor house," said Fred. "It still belongs to a certain Lord Foy. Keep well away," he added with a grimace. Something about the way he said the name "Lord Foy" struck Maggie. She glanced at the crumbling walls of the estate as they drove by. They seemed to go on and on, dark and dogged like the walls of an old fortress. For the first time since they had started driving, Fred fell briefly silent.

"Nearly there now, Maggie. See the wooden gate up there, that's us. Cherry Tree Cottage."

The tree-lined driveway was long and filled with bumps, a scattering of snow-packed gravel and deep potholes. They pulled into a clearing at the end, headlights swerving, and Maggie caught a brief glimpse of a small stone house with whitewashed walls and a thatched roof. A few candles burned inside, casting warm patches of yellow light into the darkness.

Fred got out of the Land Rover. For a moment, Maggie hesitated. Everything seemed different, so . . . *different*. She dipped her hand into her pocket for reassurance. "Thanks for coming with me," she whispered to Hurricane and Spitfire. "Although you didn't exactly have a choice, but still. I'm glad you're here."

"What did you say?" called Fred, slamming the car door.

"N-n-n-n-n-othing," said Maggie, climbing out. "Thanks. That's all."

He gave her a cheerful smile. "This way, then. The back door is round the side, past the game larder."

A clean, fresh saltiness tinged the air. Maggie

noticed it right away and wondered how close they were to the sea.

Perhaps there was something special about the air after all. She took a deep breath and glanced at the night sky. She was not used to seeing so many stars. Hundreds and thousands of them glimmered between the branches of surrounding trees. Crowns of stars. Each one impossibly bright, impossibly fierce.

# Chapter 8

The door to the flat opened. Singing. The clattering of keys into a tray. The flick of a light switch. A gasp. Then a sudden, high-pitched shriek.

Rumpus scrambled off the coffee table and hid behind an armchair.

"My curtains! Oh my goodness . . . my lamp . . . the table . . . oh . . . it's not possible!" He watched her walk slowly into the kitchen. She covered her mouth with one hand. "I don't believe this . . ." she said, her voice trailing away.

Rumpus wondered if she was going to feed him, since he hadn't actually eaten a proper dinner yet. He crept out into the center of the room.

Arabella stared at him.

"You are a monster," she whispered. "You have destroyed my flat, my furniture, my carpets! My . . ." Her gaze trailed around the room, taking in new details of destruction. "My vintage fashion magazines!"

Then she stalked back into the hallway and picked

up the phone. Her fingernails scratched the surface of the dial as it swung around and around.

"Stanley! Yes, yes, it's Arabella. Oh, Stanley!" She let out a sob. "My flat is ruined! The cat, oh, it's not a cat, it's a beast, it's a monster!" Her voice became hysterical. "You must get rid of it, Stanley. Call your driver, immediately. Get him over here now. Yes, Martin. Now! . . . I know it's eleven o'clock at night. I don't care!" She hung up.

Rumpus sniffed the air, his tail hanging low. It did not seem as though she was about to feed him.

The woman moved around in a hurry. She grabbed his lead, his water bowl, and threw them into his crate. She picked her way through the mess on the kitchen floor and over to the fridge. Rumpus followed, hoping she had at last remembered. He watched her take hold of the brown parcel, carry it over to his crate, and throw it inside. Rumpus raced after it.

Seconds later, the door slammed shut behind him.

Rumpus didn't mind because there were so many meatballs spilling out of the parcel. He ripped apart the paper and ate everything.

The woman marched about crying, her footsteps clicking and skidding across the kitchen floor.

Rumpus finished off the meatballs, licked his lips, and lay down. Then he heard a new voice, a deep voice. Somebody had come into the flat and was talking to the woman.

"Ms. Pennyworth! With all due respect, I can't just get rid of it! Where am I supposed to put it? It's a leopard! What do you want me to do? Leave it on the street in a cardboard box? It's not exactly a lost kitten!"

"Martin, there's no need to be rude. Look at the state of my flat! Look at the damage it's done . . ." Her voice cracked. She pulled out a handkerchief and dabbed her eyes. "It's actually my birthday today, Martin. Just look at me. I'm thirty years old. And this is what I'm supposed to be celebrating?"

"Oh, Ms. Pennyworth, there's no need to cry." He paused. "Let me think about this for a minute. Maybe I could drive him out of town, into the countryside perhaps. I have heard of people doing that sort of thing with these big cats. In a pinch, of course."

"Yes, oh, Martin, just drive him away. Scotland, Cornwall, I don't care. It would be better for him in the countryside anyway." Sniffles. Pause. "Yes, that's where an animal like this belongs, in a forest somewhere, not in London. I don't know what my brother was thinking. Couldn't you do that, Martin? I'll pay you of course. Double."

"All right, I'll try to find a forest or something."

"Yes." Sniffle. "A forest."

Not long afterward, Rumpus was being bounced down the stairs. Bounce, bang, bounce, bang, bounce. He skidded about as the crate was half lifted, half heaved, and half shoved out of the building and into the back of a van.

The noise of the engine was disturbing. He did not know what was going on. All he could see was the occasional flash of a passing streetlamp. Rumpus lay down and eventually fell asleep, his body lulled by the endless bumps and seams of the motorway. Occasionally he woke, not knowing where he was. In those brief seconds of reawakening, he would look for Rosie and cry out for her. But she never responded.

The night wore on, and Rumpus felt the van start to swerve. They were no longer on straight, flat roads but twisting and turning. He felt increasingly disoriented and had no sense of where he was going or why. After several hours, the car came to a slow stop. The engine kept running. He heard the man get out, footsteps skidding. A twist and a clunk. Then the van doors swung open, and he was momentarily blinded by a flash of light.

Rumpus cowered.

The man leaned forward and unlocked the crate.

"Here, kitty," he said softly. "Kitty, kitty."

Rumpus looked up but did not step forward. He tried to get a sense of this new place, but everything, absolutely everything, was strange and unfamiliar. The smells, the air, the unease in this man's voice, the quiet.

"Come on! Oh, for heaven's sake." The man lunged forward. He grabbed hold of Rumpus's collar and pulled him forward. Rumpus twisted his head. "Steady now." Rumpus did not like the feeling of being pulled by his neck. He yanked his head from side to side. The man didn't let go. "Hey! Careful! Stop that!" There was a loud ripping sound. Rumpus jumped out of the van and shook his head again and again. The collar was off!

"Finally! Go on. Get lost! GO!" The man picked up

the broken collar and hurled it into the woods. Rumpus watched as he slammed the van doors and hurried back to the driver's seat. He revved the engine and was gone, leaving Rumpus on the side of the road. Alone.

He flared his nostrils and cocked his ears, his senses tingling on alert. He peered into the darkness. A pair of snow-filled ditches lined the sides of the lane. One side backed up against the edge of a tall, dark forest. He sniffed the air. So many unfamiliar scents, noises he did not recognize. Was this a safe place? He did not know.

He decided to stay on the edge of the road and turn away from the forest. A cluster of lights glinted in the distance, and he was reminded of the department store. He would go there. Perhaps he would find a place to shelter and sleep. Perhaps he would find Rosie. He called out for her, his cries loud and insistent. Where could she be?

The night was dark, the moon hidden. Rumpus set off. His body melted into the shadowy edges of the lane like a puff of silver smoke.

He kept on crying.

# Chapter 9

Maggie woke in the middle of the night. The sound was unnerving. She didn't know what it was. There . . . she heard it again. Was it a bird? No, it was more of a howl, a kind of crying almost. She sat up and pulled back the curtains.

The moon cast just enough light for her to see that snow was falling now, soft and thick. She could see Fred's wide garden laid out below, sloping all the way down to the twisted, soft-covered branches of the apple orchard. Then something caught her attention. A movement. Something ghostly slipping through the shadows of the bare boughs, a movement so subtle she wondered if she was imagining it. An animal? Maybe . . . then it emerged, melting out of the trees. It loped silently across the lawn, moving like running water. It had a silver-gray, dappled back and the longest, fluffiest tail she had ever seen. Was it a *cat*? Maggie rubbed her eyes with both hands. But when she opened them again, the creature was gone.

The snow kept falling, whirling, and she wondered if she was, in fact, dreaming.

Early the next morning, sunlight streamed through the curtains. Maggie woke and felt curiously optimistic. Her room was small and bright, with flowery blue wallpaper and a white door. An armchair sat in one corner, piled high with bright cushions, in front of a bookshelf stuffed full of books. It felt cozy—not as cozy as her room at home, but she liked it all the same.

She threw back the covers and went straight over to the window, wondering if she had dreamt strange dreams about a mysterious creature in the moonlight or if there would be any tracks to prove it. She saw none. A fresh layer of sparkling snow covered everything from the stone wall at the end of the garden to the hedgerows in the nearby fields. All was white.

"Did either of you see anything strange last night?" she said, picking up the jar on the windowsill. The glass was cold. "I thought I saw something . . . I don't know, something weaving in between the trees," she added. "An animal maybe, silver-gray with a very long tail. It looked a bit like a cat . . . a big cat. But it wasn't as big as"—she tried to remember exactly what she had seen—"I don't know, a leopard or anything." Then she wrinkled her nose and thought for a moment that it actually *had* looked a bit like a leopard. A small silver ghost-leopard. No! Couldn't have been. She set the jar back down and opened up her suitcase.

She was digging around for her favorite wool sweater when a black-and-white photograph fluttered to the ground. The picture was of her parents and Maggie when she was very young. They were each holding one of her chubby, little hands, walking along a pebbly beach somewhere. All of them were smiling. She turned it over. On the back she read *Summer 1954. You're my girl* in her mother's neat flowing script. Maggie had no recollection of the picture being taken, where they had been or when.

It seemed strange, Father smiling like that. She didn't ever think of him as smiling, not now anyway. He always seemed so serious. Serious and tired, as if the world had been wrung out of all its beauty, leaving nothing behind to wonder at. Maggie touched the face of her mother and felt a pang of homesickness. She must have hidden the picture inside her bag on purpose, knowing it would be a happy surprise for her to find. Maggie placed the picture on her bedside table and finished getting dressed.

Fred's cottage was full of low ceilings and creaking floorboards. Every window ledge, shelf, and open nook was crammed with a collection of something or other: shells, pebbles, dried flowers, conkers, beech-nuts, acorns. She stopped at the top of the stairway and picked up a fallen bird's nest. The delicate branches felt firm and rough in her hands, woven together into a smooth, tight hollowing. He wasn't lying when he'd talked about collecting things. So much of the outside world had found its way inside the cottage, it was as if the walls of the house could breathe, blurring the two worlds together. Maggie put the nest back carefully, ducked under several exposed beams, and made her way downstairs to the kitchen. She could smell baked bread.

“Good morning, Maggie,” said Fred. “Perfect timing.” He was standing in front of a cream-colored Aga with silver-capped burners. “Sleep all right?”

“W_____w— —w— —.” She stopped and nodded instead. Her cheeks burned. She tried switching out the “w” in “well.” “Good,” she said smoothly. “I ss-s-lept good, thank you.”

Fred caught her eye. He smiled gently. She studied

the look on his face for a moment. He seemed less nervous than before, and the creases around his mouth appeared genuine.

"Have a seat. I thought you might like some breakfast." He tapped his spatula on the side of a cast-iron pan full of scrambled eggs. "These are fresh Cornish eggs, the best you'll ever eat."

Maggie nodded again. She squeezed herself onto a bench beside the window, pushing aside a heap of newspapers, books, and a pair of binoculars.

"You do like eggs, don't you?" he added. "Your mother always did, but that doesn't mean you're the same, of course."

"Y—yes. I do."

She wondered if he had remembered to call Mother but didn't want to go through the embarrassment of trying to ask, so she said nothing. Fred put the plate down in front of her, and Maggie started to eat. The eggs were bright yellow and buttery. He bustled around her, bringing over a cup of apple juice and some extra toast.

Maggie ate in silence, grateful for the effort he was making and equally grateful that he wasn't forcing her to make conversation. He seemed more comfortable with the quiet too, which was good.

She glanced out of the window. Bird feeders stood on tall slim posts outside, poking out of the snow. From the small slanted rooftops and uneven openings, Maggie could tell they were homemade. A flurry of sparrows, chaffinches, and black birds competed with one another for the seeds.

"They aren't used to this cold weather," said Fred, following her gaze. "I don't suppose any of us are. I've never seen as much snow as this, at least not in Cornwall." He sat beside her and sipped on a mug of hot tea. "How's your hand feeling? Would you like me to take a look at it?"

Maggie shook her head. "It's o-k-k—k-kay, thanks. Maybe later." She felt embarrassed suddenly and wasn't sure what he would think of her if she tried to explain what had happened.

Fred was looking at her directly. His eyes were bright and full of curiosity, as if it genuinely mattered to him how she was feeling, what she was thinking.

"Th-th-thank you." He was probably a really good doctor, she thought. Better than Nurse Nora at any rate. She glanced out of the window again. The snow looked fresh and inviting.

"C-c-c-c-c-can I g-g-go outsi-i-ide? After breakfast?" she said.

"Of course you can!" Fred put down his tea. "You're in the countryside now. You never have to ask me if it's okay to go outside. Your mother grew up outside, cartwheeling and running all over the place, barefoot to boot. Like you, I see," he said, catching sight of her bare feet beneath the table. He smiled. "You'll need shoes today though. We're still below zero, and that won't change any time soon. I promised your mother we'd keep up with your schoolwork, but you can start that in a day or two. Get used to the place first, go out, explore, go down to Wildoak if you like."

Maggie raised her eyebrows.

"Wildoak," Fred said, pointing out of the window, "is the forest over there. It's one of the last remaining pieces of ancient woodland in the whole of England."

Maggie followed the line of his finger and looked beyond the bird feeders, past the slope of the lawn, toward the brow of an adjoining hill in the distance. A crescent of tall, dark trees stood silhouetted against the pale sky, an army of gentle giants, dusted in glittering white snow.

"Although it might not be around much longer." The expression on Fred's face altered, and he muttered something under his breath. Then he added, "It's a magical place, so it is. Real magic, if you know what I mean."

Maggie wondered what he meant about real magic and thought about the ghostly creature she had glimpsed loping through the night. Fred got up and went over to the sink, tipping out the last of his tea. Maggie kept staring out the window. She had never been inside a forest before, not a real one. She had gone to Hyde Park with Mum, but that was different. There were rules there.

Fred's radio played in the background, and she caught murmurs of newscasters reporting on the Big Freeze, of people ice-skating along the River Thames, how unbelievable it all was. She continued to stare out the window, at the trees and how they reached toward the sky, impossibly tall. She felt a glimmer of possibility but hardly dared to believe it. Unbelievable things happened sometimes. Perhaps the air down here really would make a difference and her stutter would get better. Then she could forget all about Granville. She hopped up, cleared her plate, and went to find a pair of thick socks and some boots. She couldn't wait to get outside.

# Chapter 10

The twinkling lights did not look or smell anything like the Pet Kingdom. Rumpus could not find a place to shelter or sleep, nor could he find a single trace of Rosie. He kept close to the shadows and loped his way through the small cluster of streets and houses. At the far end of the village stood a manor house, larger and grander than all the others. Rumpus slipped between the bars of a spiked gate and made his way across a wide, open lawn. He did not notice the dark silhouette of a man sitting inside one of the dimly lit bedrooms. The man sucked on a pipe. His face was cut out of the light, and smoke encircled his head like a self-made crown.

Rumpus carried on. He was tired and confused. The manor house made no sense to him, and he left as easily as he had come. With the village now behind him, he turned down a narrow country lane and wandered past a lopsided gate and whitewashed cottage. He stopped to sniff the air at the edge of an apple orchard. The night was quiet. It began to snow again. He had no sense of this land, no sense of where he belonged here. He wanted to find Rosie and didn't understand what had happened. He called out for her one last time.

Still, she did not come.

The snow continued to whirl. He left the orchard and headed toward the line of trees on the far side of a small valley. He had come full circle now and did not know where else to go.

He had never walked into a forest before. All of his senses sharpened on instinct. His nostrils flared and his ears pricked up. The smell of the earth, hard-packed and frozen, the dampness of snow-covered bark, the fresh scent of an unfamiliar marking and the almost-imperceptible sound of wings beating overhead. A growing array of new voices confused him. His presence triggered a variety of calls, some alarmed, others curious. These sounds were all new to him, and he was not sure if he was welcome in this place or not.

The snow fell harder now, in heavy sweeps. He moved softly, following a narrow path that led him deeper into the forest until it pooled into a small circular clearing. Rumpus stopped. In the center of the clearing stood an enormous tree, laden with snow. The trunk was thick and split down the middle, blasted apart by lightning. But somehow it had survived and continued to grow, its limbs hanging down like the arms of a sleeping giant.

Rumpus approached the tree cautiously, sniffed and listened, flipping his ears independently. Then he scaled one of the low-slung branches, his claws sinking into the rugged bark. Once high enough, he could see down into the open heart of the blackened trunk. His tail flicked from side to side. The remains of a squirrel dray lay scattered inside the hollowing, but otherwise it was empty and secluded. He lowered himself down, curled up, and wrapped his tail around his body like a blanket. This was a safe place.

When he woke, Rumpus found his head pressed against the insides of the trunk. A centipede snaked her way past the tip of his nose, her tiny footsteps no more than whispered vibrations. He sat up and yawned. His tongue felt dry, and he was hungry. He peered out of the hollow and looked around, moving his head very slowly. Early morning light had crept into the snow-covered clearing. The edges of things glittered. A cold breeze ruffled the fur on the back of his head.

He did not know where or how to find meat-balls here.

Something caught his eye, and he looked up. A squirrel stood, poised on the tip of a narrow branch, clasping an acorn between his paws. His head was cocked to one side, and he stared at Rumpus in shock. Rumpus yawned again. The squirrel bolted. Unable to resist a chase, Rumpus leapt out of the hol-lowing. He scrambled from branch to branch, but the squirrel was nimble and quick. Rumpus retreated, the slimmer branches sagging beneath his weight.

The sun continued to rise, and before long, the whole clearing was bathed in light. Crystals of snow and frost glittered; droplets dripped. Rumpus sat among the thick, twisted roots of the ancient tree. He did not yet feel comfortable in this place but was aware that others did. The longer he lay still, the more the birds returned to whatever it was they had been doing. Their flutes, curls, and chattering wove an invisible web of song into the sky. The surrounding trees stood beside one another, their tall branches intermingling like the tips of long, slender fingers, their roots clasped in a slowly expanding embrace. This forest was a place like no other.

Without warning, the birds suddenly erupted into a loud, anxious chattering. Rumpus put his nose in the air. He caught a whiff of something and instinctively flattened himself to the ground. Perhaps he was not the only one chasing squirrels.

A flash of dark orange, pointed ears, brush tail. The fox ran between the trees. When she emerged just a few feet away, she took one look in his direction, then disappeared. Rumpus stood. She had been smaller than he. He wasn't sure if he should try to chase her too, or if she was friendly and might like to play. He bounded after her for a moment but soon changed his mind. His mouth was still dry. He needed a drink.

He left the clearing and went in search of water. His wide, flat paws worked well on the fresh snow, and it was easy to stay hidden as he moved softly between the fragments of shifting light and shadow.

He almost didn't see the hedgehog until he was upon it.

Surprised, the hedgehog immediately formed a small spiky ball, her spines protruding at all angles. Rumpus was not sure if she was trying to play. He was also not sure if he should try to eat her. He batted her with his paw, just to see what would happen. She rolled sideways. Delighted, he batted her with his other paw. The hedgehog rolled again. Rumpus sprang back with excitement. This was like the game he used to play with Rosie, although their ball had been much softer. The hedgehog squeaked. Rumpus dived forward, rolling her from side to side. The hedgehog tightened her roll-up. But the more she rolled and bounced about, the more he played with her, until he opened his jaws spontaneously and tried to pick her up. Her spines pricked his tongue and stabbed the roof of his mouth. Disgusted, he half sneezed and half spat her out again. He screwed up his face, curling back his lips. She did not taste or feel anything like a meatball.

Offended by the needling cuts all over his tongue, Rumpus left the hedgehog by the side of the path and carried on. Now he wanted a drink more than ever. He made his way to the edge of the forest and came across a narrow, frozen stream. There were breaks in the ice, and he drank thirstily. The water tasted sharp and refreshing. It also numbed his tongue.

Rumpus was still drinking when he sensed the light vibration of footsteps. He stopped, water dripping from his chin. Human footsteps, too light for a man. He looked up and scanned his surroundings. He spotted a girl, a hundred yards or so upstream, running up the bank.

Rumpus backed away slowly in a kind of reverse stalk. He was no longer sure about humans. Maybe she would have meatballs, but maybe she would try to put him back in a crate, or worse.

He retreated into the forest.

# Chapter 11

The entrance to Wildoak was no more than a narrow wooden stile. Maggie climbed it easily. Once among the tall, broad trees, she couldn't help but look up. It felt as though she had walked into a magnificent open-air cathedral. The air was quiet and still. Sunlight fell from the sky in bars of gold light. Frost and ice slipped from the tips of branches and fell onto her shoulders. She inhaled the crisp, cool air, the smell of damp earth and fresh snow. Time was kept differently here.

Her boots squeaked against the hard-packed ground as she followed a loose path forward. She walked on, feeling her cheeks grow pink with cold. For a moment she paused at the base of an especially thick beech. The tree's trunk was so broad she could not wrap her arms around it, so tall she could not see its top. Maggie took the mitten off her good hand and reached out to touch the damp stony-brown bark. The surface felt old and rough beneath her palm, like the hide of some ancient animal, thickly skinned. Something about the aliveness of the thing, the slow and steady being of it, surprised her. She put her ear to it, curious if she might be able to hear something. She could not, but she stayed for a few minutes, wondering.

The path carried on, deeper into the forest. Occasionally Maggie stopped to stomp on one of the really big icy puddles, fracturing the crusty surface like a thick plate of tinkling glass. The path eventually came to a dead end at a small, round clearing. Maggie paused. In the center of the clearing was a massive ancient oak tree, wild in every way. Split down the center, it had been lashed by lightning, wind, and rain; nourished and cracked by the sun and felted in patches of ice-encrusted moss. Several branches hung down, like the open arms of a sleeping giant, his knuckles grazing the snowy ground. Maggie had not climbed a tree before, but that was exactly what she wanted to do. Climb. Ignoring the cold, she took off her boots and socks and tried to find her footing amid the labyrinth of thick, wild roots and knotted burls. The bark was rough and crumbly beneath her bare feet. She clambered upward, grasping fistfuls of damp, tangled ivy. She climbed until she was high enough to peer inside the hollow.

The insides of the tree were smooth in part, the bark pulled tight like scar tissue. It was open and dry, empty except for the remnants of an old nest of sorts. Her heart beat a little harder, a little faster. And she felt it again, that strange sense of aliveness, as if the old tree was properly alive. Alive like her.

She looked up at the branches and thought about Flute and how much he would love this tree, this place. Wellington too, all the little nooks and crannies he would be able to curl up in. She missed them keenly.

Maggie sat down and dangled her feet into the hollow. Her toes had turned pink and were almost numb with cold. Branches felt their way into the air above and all around her. She lay back and felt held by the tree, cradled by it. Maybe the air here was healing. Maybe her stutter really would go away, once and for all.

She sat up, hit by a sudden wave of impatience. It just wasn't fair. Why should she be sitting in this tree, hoping for some kind of miracle, when everyone else was going to school, saying whatever they wanted, whenever they felt like it? Why did she have to wrestle with feeling scared every time she opened her mouth, scared of being sent to some place that tied children down, starved them, frightened them? All of these emotions crowded into the space around her heart like a throat full of fists, pressing up against the insides of her chest. Pressing hard. She closed her eyes.

Then an odd thing happened.

Maggie wasn't sure if the branch was faintly trembling or if something inside her was. But for a moment she felt a kind of energy flow through her, a not-quite vibration of something.

*Be*

*gentle*

*with*

*yourself.*

*It*

*is*

*hard*

*to be*

*human.*

She did not hear these words, or see them, but they echoed in the back of her mind somewhere, fading in and out, burning at the edges.

Was the tree speaking to her? No, that was impossible. Trees didn't talk.

But the words printed themselves on the insides of her heart, soft as butterfly wings.

*Be gentle with yourself. It is hard to be human.*

Maggie gripped the sides of the branch she was sitting on. She opened her eyes wide and looked around. Was somebody else here?

No . . . The clearing was quiet and empty. She shivered. Where the message had come from, she didn't know, but it comforted her. She wriggled her toes. They had stiffened with cold. Maybe she was so cold she was hearing things?

She started to climb back down. She wanted to put on her boots again and was half thinking about lunch when there was a sudden sharp *crack*. A snap. A rustle.

Maggie stopped mid-climb, half hanging from a branch. The hair along the nape of her neck quivered. She let go and landed with a thump. For a second, she thought she saw something, a rippling alongside the edge of the clearing.

"Wh-wh-wh-who's th-ere?" she called out. "Is s-s-s-somebody th-ere?"

No answer.

"H-h-h-ello?" she tried again.

Silence.

She put on her socks and boots quickly. Something or somebody was watching her, she could feel it. But when she went to part the brush, nobody was there.

Maggie got back to the house and found a note on the kitchen table. *Hope you like sandwiches. Am working in shed. Come and find me when you're back. I've got something for you. —Fred*

Next to the note was a plate with a sandwich on it. Maggie peeled back one of the thick, fluffy slices of bread. Cheese and Branston Pickle, her favorite.

The kitchen felt warm and inviting after so much cold. The shelves were stacked with blue-and-white-striped plates, most of them chipped, a collection of egg cups and mismatched mugs. Tattered cookbooks lay around, the pages dog-eared and worn. Tea towels with hens printed on them hung beside the Aga. Maggie took a bite of her sandwich and wondered if Fred ever got lonely here. It didn't seem that way. Mum had said he'd been living alone for almost twenty years, since

Grandma had died, and he was used to it now. But still, photos of her were dotted all over the house alongside several of Mother as a child and one or two of Maggie when she was a baby. It struck her as sad that Mother only spoke to him on the phone and hadn't seen him for so long. She wondered what exactly had happened to cause such a terrible row with Father.

Maggie picked up her sandwich and ate hungrily, the pickle tangy and sweet alongside the salty cheddar. She wasn't sure whether or not it would be rude to ask Fred why he and Father hadn't spoken to each other for such a long time. It didn't make any sense. The words *it is hard to be human* echoed quietly in the back of her mind. Perhaps she should tell him about that too, her feeling that she had sort-of heard the old tree speak. She decided not to. He might think she was a bit strange or a maybe a bit mad . . . if he didn't already.

Wzzzzzzzwhzzzzzzzz. WHRRRRRRRRZZZZZZZz. The sounds coming from inside the shed were loud and unfamiliar. Maggie tentatively pushed open one of the sliding doors. Inside, the shed was dark and cluttered, the shelves overloaded with tools, grungy oil cans, and bits of half-dismantled things, like lawn mower engines and bike chains.

"H-hi."

Fred had his back to the door. Sparks flew. He was cutting something with a wheel saw and didn't hear her. Maggie gently touched his shoulder.

"H—Hi, G-G-G-G-G-G___________G_G—" she repeated. She decided to just call him "Fred" as he'd suggested.

Fred turned. He was wearing goggles and had bits of sawdust stuck in his hair.

"Hi, Maggie! How was your morning? Did you find the sandwich I left for you?"

Direct questions often flustered her, and she knew before she even tried to answer that the words wouldn't come. She tried coughing, but her head started to jerk before she could open her mouth. "Y-y-y." Block. "Y-e." Block. She felt her head jerk and jerk and jerk until finally it stopped and she could take a long breath in.

"I'm sure you did, love," he said gently. "Come over here. I've got a surprise for you."

Maggie followed him to the other side of the bench. She looked at the back of his head and shoulders, at his disheveled white hair, and felt a pang of gratitude.

"I'm rather proud of this old girl, I must say," Fred went on. He pointed to a large silver contraption. There was a bicycle seat, a steering wheel, possibly from a car, and three sets of "feet." The back two were longer flat pieces of silver metal, smooth along the edges. The front was shorter and looked like the tip of an old wooden ski.

"Wh-wh-what . . . is it?"

"Here," said Fred, leaning forward and lifting it up with both arms. "Come with me and I'll show you. You might like to try it."

They walked out to the top of the hill. She could see it now. It was a sled. Fred motioned for her to climb on if she wanted, and she did. She gripped the wheel with both mittens as best she could. The slope down to the bottom of the garden looked enormous from up here, enormous and steep.

"There are brakes, remember," said Fred, smiling.

Maggie nodded, unconvinced.

"You ready, then?"

"I think s-so."

For a moment, she sat on the brow of the hill, anticipation bristling along the nape of her neck. Fred gave her a slight push. The tip of the front sawn-off ski inched forward, pressing a fresh track into the snow. He pushed a little more. It creaked. Maggie leaned back, and the metal feet glided forward slowly, slowly, until suddenly she was out over the edge of the hill.

The sled took off.

She gasped.

A bomb of fear exploded inside the pit of her stomach and she rocketed downward. It didn't seem possible to go any faster. The wind whipped her face. Her hat flew off. She screamed, but the screams bubbled into whoops of laughter and she didn't know if she was loving it or hating it until she had careened to the bottom, swerving wildly at the last second to avoid crashing into the stream.

Fred came running down to meet her.

"What a ride, Maggie!"

Maggie was gasping for breath. She was half laughing, half shaking.

"You okay?" he asked.

A huge smile slowly spread across her face.

"I. I. I th-th-th-think so."

Fred laughed. He held her hand, and they pulled the sled back to the top of the hill together. Maggie took turn after turn after turn, still not sure if she was loving or hating it.

# Chapter 12

The sun hung high in the sky, well past noon. Rumpus felt his belly rumble. He was used to being fed at the same time each day, once in the morning and once at night. The girl had not been carrying meatballs earlier, at least none that he could smell. He bounded through the forest, sniffing, listening, looking. There was still so much to understand. So much to explore. And chase, from the furry-tailed squirrels to the velvety-backed voles.

He lifted his chin in the air, trying to get a sense of how the wind was blowing. He headed east, springing between the trees and occasionally stopping to pounce on a rustling leaf.

The pile of small, shiny pebbly droppings lay at the base of a large beech. They smelled different from his own scat. Grassy, sour. Rumpus pawed at the little pellets, scattering them in all directions. Then he took another deep sniff. He did not know what a roe deer was, but it didn't matter. What mattered was disguising himself. He lay down on one side and rolled into the pellets, turning onto his back and waving his paws in the air. Then he wriggled from side to side, pressing his fur into the dung, rubbing himself into it. When he got up, some of the pellets had stuck to his back. That was better. Nobody would be able to pick up his scent now. He could stalk in secret.

Rumpus picked his way between the trees, in search of another squirrel. He kept catching whiffs of them. His belly rumbled again. Just the thought of eating was enough to make his mouth water.

Something flickered in the corner of his eye, and he turned. A plump bird with a long copper-colored tail was running, darting between the trees. The pheasant's dark-velvet-green head bobbed as it ran, its bright red eye patch flashing from side to side. Rumpus chased it, springing and leaping easily over fallen logs. The pheasant squawked with alarm, flapping and shrieking. With his front paws outstretched, Rumpus made a desperate attempt to catch up. He jumped, sailing into the air but landed wide with a noisy crash. The pheasant took flight. Rumpus sprang back up.

A flood of alarm calls from other pheasants filled the air, all flapping and screeching. He would not catch anything now. He turned around and went in search of a quieter spot where different tactics might work better.

The old stump was covered in moss and patches of snow. The very tips of a few small snowdrops peeked out nearby. Rumpus crouched behind the stump and flattened himself. This would make a good hiding spot. If another small furry creature passed by, he would be able to pounce on short notice. He lay in wait for a while, the breeze ruffling his soft gray fur.

The sun inched its way into the afternoon. He remained as still and quiet as he possibly could. The birds resumed their business. Melting snow dribbled down the side of the stump and occasionally fell from nearby branches with a powdery thud. He swatted at them with his paw. No squirrels came. He was about to lose patience when the ground started to shake. The tremor was faint at first, but then it got stronger and closer. Too close. He leapt up, scrambling into the nearest tree. He made it to the lower-level branches just as an open-topped truck bounced down the track. The smell of the exhaust stung his nostrils.

Two men sat in the front of the car. The driver was short and heavyset. He gripped the steering wheel with both hands, tight. The other man was tall and thin, with hunched shoulders. The gleaming barrels of a shotgun rested across his lap. A collection of strange-looking equipment bounced in the back of the truck: rolls of paper, prongs with silver dials, metal boxes, cables, and wires.

Rumpus waited until they had passed before he climbed down. It might be safer to return to the clearing with an empty stomach. On his way back, he paused to sharpen his claws against the base of an old ash. He spied a large black beetle trundling up one side of the tree and pinned it. The beetle twitched beneath his paw. It did not taste good, wriggling and crispy inside his mouth, but it was better than nothing.

He was not far from the clearing when a series of strange sounds struck him. He pricked his ears. Whoops and screams. Human laughter, loud. Something swishing and gliding at high speed. It sounded like the girl. The noises were confusing. Was she in danger?

He carried on, picking his pathway through the trees and heavy brush, still listening, still trying to figure out what was going on.

He did not look down.

He did not see the metal plate, concealed as it was beneath so much snow.

*Pop.*

The spring made a quiet popping sound as it released. The shock of it was instant. Rumpus jumped straight up in the air but was immediately yanked back down. His body fell, buckling sideways. The jaws of the trap engulfed his paw. The pain was electric. He hissed and growled, bucked and pulled, but couldn't make it stop. Agony swept up his leg and shoulder. He mouthed at the trap, gripped it, bit at it, but no matter what he tried, he could not get it off his paw. The sharp metal teeth pressed tight and deep. The trap had been staked to the ground. He did not understand what was happening or why.

Eventually, Rumpus collapsed on the snow-cold earth. He lay there, unable to move until darkness enveloped the sky and he could no longer fight the pain.

# Chapter 13

Maggie watched her grandfather load up the fireplace, her cheeks still red with windburn. The flames flickered and curled upward, heating the small sitting room. She sat on one of the sofas, under a moth-eaten blanket, her hands wrapped around a warm mug. It was almost dark outside, and she had just finished two bowls of hot stew and dumplings.

"Well, seems to me you'll be ready to drive a car in no time," said Fred, dusting the ash off his hands and coming to sit beside her. "It's not all that different from driving a sled, you know. Point in the direction you want to go, brake, steer a bit, go some more, brake some more. Fewer hills of course."

Maggie wondered if Fred was the best person to be taking driving advice from, but she smiled anyway. She noticed that he had started talking to her without asking so many direct questions. There were even a few stretches of comfortable silence between them now. She sat back a bit and took a sip of the hot chocolate he had made for her. It was bitter and sweet at the same time and warmed her stomach.

"I'm proud of that sled," Fred added. "I've made some fine things in my time, but I must say she's one of the finest." He looked sideways at Maggie and winked. "*And* you're still in one piece."

"What else have you m—made?" Maggie asked. She loved the way Fred's shirt collar always seemed to poke out of his sweater all crumpled and his hair was never properly combed.

"Oh, I'm always working on one thing or another." He settled back into his chair and put up his feet. His argyle socks were bright red and damp at the toes. "Not all of them have been"—he cleared his throat—"well, successful. Although that might depend on your definition of 'success,' if you know what I mean. The Berry Pickers were good. Mechanical gloves with little pincers at the end of each fingertip. I love jam, you see, and pick a lot of blackberries. But it takes a long time and you get pricked by all the thorns. Problem was the pincers kept getting, uh, *jammed*."

Maggie rolled her eyes at the pun but couldn't help laughing.

"A-a—anything else?" she said.

"Hmmmm." Fred took another sip of his tea. "Let me think. The see-in-the-dark goggles were a bit of a disaster. Oh, and what did I call it, ah yes, the kite camera—that almost worked. But I never managed to get the clicker right, and the neighbors got annoyed with the kite hovering all over the place. But the one I'm really excited about, the biggest and the best . . . well, it's my most ambitious project yet," he said, looking at her. "Promise you won't tell anyone?"

Maggie nodded. Fred leaned a little closer and dropped his voice to a whisper. "It's a flying automobile."

Maggie's eyebrows shot up. "A f—-f-lying ca-a-ar?"

"Well, you can't call yourself an inventor and not have a crack at your own flying machine of one sort or another!" Fred leaned back, folding his arms in satisfaction. "I've a long way to go yet, and it's harder to work on it in the winter of course. Mind you, in sixty-three years, we have never had a winter like this."

Maggie had so many questions. How had he come up with such a wild idea? When would it be ready to try out? Had he made wings? Most families on Methley

Street didn't have cars, at least that she knew of, and the idea of one that could fly struck her as thrilling and completely mad at the same time. She was about to ask, but she felt a sudden wave of exhaustion, and asking anything out loud was even harder when she was tired. She finished her drink and picked up an old newspaper and pen. Above Fred's half-completed crossword, she wrote:

*Thank you for today. I loved it. Thank you for being so kind to me. Good night.* She underlined the phrase "I loved it" and then handed the paper to Fred.

Fred got up and put his arms out as if he was going to hug her but then wasn't sure if he could or should and changed his mind at the last moment, stepping back. She waited patiently.

"Maggie, I've been alone for many years," he said. The fire snapped and flickered. "Having you here, spending this time with you"—he paused—"brings me great joy."

Then she hugged him anyway, a strong, bony-armed hug. His sweater smelled of woodsmoke. And he hugged her back, tight.

"Night, then," he said. "I'll see you in the morning." She kept her arms around him a moment longer, saying the things she wanted to say without using any words at all.

Maggie closed her door and flopped onto the bed. The photograph of her parents was where she had left it, propped beside the lamp. She stared at it. Her father looked so happy and relaxed in the picture, but he never looked like that now. Maggie tried to imagine him smiling at her like that but couldn't. When had he gone from that person to the one who was always so serious and tired?

She rolled over with a sigh. Even though the sledding had been so much fun, she felt a heaviness settle inside her chest. She had not been able to speak to Fred without stuttering. So far, nothing had changed.

*Be gentle with yourself. It is hard to be human.*

The words of the ancient oak came back to her again. She wasn't sure she completely understood the message . . . but it calmed her now, and she felt some of the tightness in her chest and shoulders soften.

The next day was Monday. Maggie went down to breakfast, carrying the jar of snails. She was a bit worried about Hurricane. She had woken to find his antennae drooping. Perhaps she shouldn't have left the snails on the windowsill when it was so cold outside. Either way, he didn't look his usual self. Hopefully it was just too much cold, but she wasn't sure.

Fred was already sitting at the kitchen table. He looked smarter than usual in a shirt that was actually ironed and a green sweater with elbow patches. A black stethoscope hung round his neck. He was reading the newspaper with a cup of tea in one hand and a piece of toast in the other. She noticed the toast was dripping with blackberry jam. A big splodge fell onto his plate.

"Mor-n-n-n-n-ing, Fred," she said.

She put the jar of snails on the table and gently nudged it toward him.

"Good morning, Maggie," he said, putting down the paper. "I hope you slept well. Ah, what do we have here? A pair of terrestrial pulmonated gastropod mollusks . . . *Cornu aspersum*. Otherwise known as the 'common garden snail.' And a handsome pair at that, although"—he put on his glasses and peered at the jar more closely—"this fellow seems a little droopy." Fred looked up. "Let's keep them down here for a bit. It's warmer in the kitchen. He probably just needs a fresh meal and some extra moisture. I'll see what I can find for him in the larder." Maggie smiled at him. He knew so much about snails!

Fred returned a few moments later with some cabbage leaves. "Here you go, try this. And then I've got to get to work, unfortunately. Lots of coughs and colds that need taking care of in this weather. I'll be back around five."

"Wh-wh-wh-ww-wh-wh-hat?" said Maggie, surprised. It hadn't occurred to her that Fred would be going to work. Or that she might be left at the house alone.

"The office is just outside Truro, not too far," he added. "And speaking of doctor's work, let me take a quick look at your hand before I go."

The bandage around Maggie's palm was now gray and frayed at the edges. Fred slowly peeled it off. "Looks good," he said. "It's starting to heal just fine. I don't think you need this thing on anymore. Give it another day or two, and we'll have those stitches out in no time."

"O-k-k-k—" Maggie tried to say. But within a syllable she felt the air catch and her throat block. "K-k-k-k__________." Block. Her head jerked suddenly. "K——ay."

Fred looked at her closely. "You sure you're okay here?" he said. She nodded. "Listen," he said, reaching into a cluttered drawer and fishing out a pen. "Here's my telephone number. You can always call the receptionist if you need me. The telephone is in the sitting room, next to the stripey armchair."

Maggie stared at the scrap of paper. The last time she had picked up a telephone, none of her words had come out. Not even the beginning parts. It was the worst block she'd ever had, and she had not been able to pick up a telephone since. She felt a wave of shame.

"All right?" Fred repeated. Maggie nodded again, as forcefully as she could. "I'll try to get back a little early."

Maggie sat at the kitchen table for a while after Fred had left. The cottage felt very quiet. She studied Hurricane and took a long deep breath. He had discovered the cabbage and seemed to be eating, which was a relief.

"What is wrong with me, Hurricane?" she whispered. "Why is it that I can talk to you and Spitfire, but not to people, and definitely not on a telephone?" *It's so hard.* For a moment, she imagined herself tied to a bed in a room full of crying children while an army of Nurse Noras marched up and down, yelling and shouting at everyone to shut up and be quiet.

The snails kept munching. Maggie turned to look out the window in an effort to think about something other than Granville. Robins, coal tits, and starlings fluttered around Fred's rickety old feeders, scrambling for food, trying to survive in all this cold.

It was not yet nine in the morning. The whole day lay ahead. Part of her wanted to sled, but she wasn't sure about going alone. She thought about returning to the forest, to visit the old oak tree again. Maybe she could play in the snow down there, or build a den?

Her gaze drifted past the birds, to the crest of the hill beyond, where the trees stood tall. Then she suddenly remembered the feeling that somebody else had been there too. Watching her. Hiding.

# Chapter 14

Rumpus lay on his side, as still as he could. Any movement, no matter how slight, wreaked agony throughout his body. He could no longer sense the sharp stabbing pains inside his paw. His soft black pads had gone numb. His fur was matted with blood and dirt.

He drifted in and out of consciousness, swinging wildly between fear and resignation. Strange shapes and shadows seemed to sway in the darkness. Were they creatures? Would they prey on him? Would they help him? He did not know. He drifted away again.

Dawn was about to break when he heard a rustling nearby. He opened his eyes and sniffed the air. His pupils dilated automatically. He could see in the dim light but could not move his head; even the slightest of movements seemed overwhelming. More rustling, louder now, closer. A strong musky scent. Bitter. Some animal was approaching from behind. The steps were heavy, low to the ground, and sturdy.

Every sense flickered into life. Rumpus forced himself to sit up, dragging his injured paw sideways. He winced. Then he caught sight of a pointed black-and-white-striped face, small white-tipped ears, and puffs of breath. He had never seen a badger before and didn't know if she would be friendly or not. She smelled of milk and something else . . . newborns? Cubs?

She was strong, with stout, thick paws and short, sharp claws. He paid close attention to the way she moved, to their shared language of face and body. She put her nose in the air and sniffed, then turned her head toward him directly. Her small black eyes traveled down to his bloodied paw, to the teeth of the trap, the rusted chain, and then the stake.

She came a little closer.

Rumpus lay back down and lowered his head. If she decided to attack, he knew instinctively that he would lose.

She came closer still.

He watched her.

She approached his injured paw. She was so close now that the tip of her nose brushed against his fur. For a moment, Rumpus thought he could see her top lip curl and abruptly tried to yank his paw backward, afraid she might bite him. The chain clanked and jangled, and she shied away. Rumpus hissed. A fresh wave of pain swept up his leg.

Slowly, the badger came back. Rumpus lay still, his body limp. He flicked his tail from side to side but was too exhausted to protest further. She crept forward. She did not attack him. She licked his wound. Gently. Bits of leaves, clumps of earth, blood, and dirt were caught in the teeth of the trap. She cleaned them all away.

Rumpus did not know how long she stayed with him. The pain was overwhelming, and he drifted away again.

The next time he opened his eyes, the badger was gone. Shafts of early morning sunlight shone between the trees, breaking apart the night. The hurt in his leg had not changed. His tongue was swollen and dry. He shifted his head to one side and tried to lick some of the hard-packed snow. It tasted earthy and gritty, but the moisture provided a little relief. He lay down again, exhausted.

Rumpus did not know how much longer he could endure the pain. His wound was wet and weeping. He could smell his own blood.

# Chapter 15

The forest was awake by the time Maggie got there. Mid-morning light crept along the snow-coated branches. A handful of birds chattered to one another. Rustlings laced the air as she headed to the clearing. The path felt more familiar this time, and Maggie noticed a slight spring in her step. She found the hollowed-out oak tree without a problem. The old giant seemed to welcome her now, with its low-hanging shaggy limbs spread out and open. It seemed like a great spot for den-building.

Maggie skimmed the clearing, searching for some solid sticks. Frost and snow glistened around her. Sturdy branches were harder to find than she expected, and she soon ventured deeper into the forest, hoping to discover more.

Her boots slid over the ice-packed floor as she picked through the rambling bracken and bursts of bare hazel. It was not easy going. She came across an enormous, fallen beech tree with all of its roots still intact, forming one massive pad of shaggy, earth-matted hair. She was trying to climb over it when she noticed a hole, set back between a cluster of the torn-up roots. It seemed large for a rabbit. Perhaps it was a fox den, or a badger sett maybe. Maggie loved badgers and always thought of them as friendly, probably because of Badger in *Wind in the Willows*. Either way, she didn't want to disturb whoever might be inside, so she turned and headed in a different direction.

She came across several longer sticks but most were wet and snapped easily in her hands. Perhaps a snow fort would be better. Maggie was wondering which would be best when she became aware of the creeping feeling that she might be lost. Things were starting to look the same no matter which direction she turned. She tried looking up, but that was no help either. A handful of crows hopped among the branches above, their silhouettes jet black against the pale sky. They were being very noisy. She tried to ignore the panicky feeling that was slowly building inside her chest. "Think," she said. "Look at the direction of the sun, turn, maybe . . . this way?" Taking a guess, she circled and walked in what she hoped might be west. She was still not sure how she would ever find her way back to the clearing when a strange streak of red caught her eye. The color was so bright and unexpected against the pale white snow.

"Oh *no,*" she whispered.

Just a few feet away lay the body of a huge silver-gray cat. There was something awful about the way he was twisted on one side. She inched forward cautiously. Blood, darker splashes were everywhere. She felt her breath catch.

*This was the ghostly creature she had seen from her bedroom.* She was sure of it, the silver-gray fur, the long, long tail. But his head was down, and he looked stiff.

Maggie's gaze followed the line of his shoulder and the strange angle of his front leg. She let out a small gasp. The cat's right paw had been clamped into the jaws of a large metal trap. She could see the teeth of the thing mashed into his fur, squashing it so hard that flesh bulged out the other side, like a swollen pouch. A heavy metal chain snaked its way through the dirty snow, staked at one end and driven deep into the hard earth. She felt a punch of nausea.

"What happened to you?" she whispered, getting down on her knees. "Oh, what is this cruel thing?" She wiped her cheeks furiously.

*Stop crying!*

The cat's eyes were closed. She ripped off one of her mittens and put the palm of her good hand in front of his nose, longing to feel breath.

He was breathing, but barely. The trap. She had to get it off. She wanted to turn away but forced herself to look. It was shaped like an iron pan, with a long handle down one side. There must be a release clip or something. Oh, the pain of it! Hurry. Surely it's not fixed shut like this? Think, Maggie. Her heart was beating so fast, it seemed to thump against her eardrums. Pull yourself together. She stood up impatiently. "Fred's toolshed. That's it. I'll cut it off." She swung round. Everything looked the same. Was it left or right?

"WHICH WAY?" she yelled.

A cold gust of wind blew through the forest. The trees swayed, sounding low notes of an ancient music. Maggie turned on instinct and ran. She ran in as straight a line as best she could, leaping over branches and fallen logs, ducking between bushes and thickets.

She ran blindly, trusting in something she couldn't see or name. Something she wasn't even sure existed.

Eventually, she broke out of the undergrowth and hit the path she had come in on. With relief, she recognized the way. Mark it, she thought quickly, mark it or she'd never find him again. She tore off her hat and dropped it on the ground. *Come on.* Then she ran all the way to the edge of the forest, over the stream, and up to Fred's toolshed.

The heavy wood doors were closed but not locked. Maggie did not know where to begin. The place was a mess. There were half-finished projects everywhere, sheets draped, machines in bits, wires, engines, tools, just a mess. She searched frantically.

"Scissors, no! Screwdriver, no! Hammer . . . maybe? NO. Bicycle chain, pedal, no, broom handle, no . . . no. Come *on*, there must be something!" She looked to the walls. Cords, ropes, pegs. Higher. Shelves so high she couldn't even see what was on them. She scrambled up onto the workbench and leaned sideways. Nothing but boxes of nails and screws. She hopped down again and turned furiously to a series of crates beneath the workbench. Oily cloths, garden shears not strong enough.

Then she saw them. Above the main doors, a pair of long-armed metal shears. They looked like giant scissors with a small, thick head. Yes! She poked at them with a shovel until they flipped off the hook and clattered to the floor. These things would cut it off. She paused. But then what? What about the wound . . . ? She would need water, the bucket . . . antiseptic . . . somewhere she had seen a first aid kit—hadn't she? She returned to the crates beneath Fred's bench and rummaged through the boxes. Tucked inside one of them was a large black tin with THE HOME FIRST AID CABINET written on it. Not much was inside except for a few bandages and a pair of tweezers. It would have to do.

Maggie struggled to cross the stream without dropping anything. The bridge across was little more than a narrow plank, and she nearly slipped. Once across, she filled the bucket and half ran, half walked as quickly as she could back into the forest. Her own hand was still sore, and now it throbbed from the pressure of carrying such a heavy load. The icy water sloshed and spilled. She was sweating by the time she got to her hat and turned off the path.

The cat was exactly where she had left him.

His eyes were still closed.

Her heart thumped.

"I've come back for you," she said. "I'm going to get you out of this thing, I swear I am."

Maggie ran her fingers over the top and sides of the trap. But where to cut? She followed the lines of steel along the handle and found a coiled spring. Was it the spring that was keeping the jaws of the trap closed? It must be. She picked up the cutters with her bare hands. They were long and unwieldy but came apart easily. Gripping as best she could, she positioned the blades around the only part of the spring coil narrow enough. She pressed down hard, harder still.

*Come on! PLEASE.*

Nothing.

She tried again, straining every muscle in both forearms, putting the weight of her shoulders and upper back into it, pressing down again and again. But the cutters barely made a dent in the rusted steel. She kept trying. She pressed with all her might. Her cheeks turned red. But no matter how hard she tried, the steel coil remained intact.

In a fit of anger, Maggie threw the cutters away.

The cat still had not moved.

"Don't give up on me," she whispered. She got back down on her hands and knees. There must be a way. Her mind spun in circles. How would a hunter get it off? She reached forward and tried again to understand how the trap worked, the mechanics of it. If only Fred were nearby, surely he would know.

Impatiently Maggie ran her finger along the handle and back again. "It's just a spring," she whispered. "Right now it's extended. *Think, Maggie.* If there's a way to extend it, there must be a way to compress it again." She studied the shape of it, the way the pieces all fit together. "What's that ring . . . ? It slides . . . there! THERE!" she said. She shifted a small iron loop. "Yes, come on!" Maggie pushed the loop as far as possible and slipped her fingers around the cold rusted metal. Then she squeezed the two handle rods like a pair of tongs. The jaws of the trap edged apart. She squeezed a little harder.

# Chapter 16

Rumpus felt a splash of cold water on his face. Was he swimming? He could hear something, but it was far away. His eyes flickered. More cold water. A shock of water. Some of it went up his nose. He coughed and opened his eyes. He was not swimming. He was in the forest and he was in pain.

The blurry world sharpened into focus. His nostrils flared. The girl from the clearing. She crouched beside him, a bucket in her hands.

Rumpus dragged himself up and tried to back away from her. A flash of fresh pain soared up his leg. He jerked and looked down. His paw was bandaged. He nipped at it immediately and tried to get the strips off. The girl started talking, her voice gentle and calm. He stopped pulling at the bandage and looked at her. She pushed the bucket of water forward, slowly, tipping it toward him.

Rumpus sniffed the rim of the bucket and leaned down. Fresh, cold water. He drank thirstily, his long pink tongue lapping and lapping. It tasted so good, clean and crisp. He finished and pulled his head back out, whiskers and chin dripping. The girl was staring at him. He hesitated. Her eyes were not threatening. The scent of her reminded him of another human, somebody from a long, long time ago, when he had been first born. Something about her eyes, dark and gentle, and her hands, tentative and soft, gave him the feeling that he was being cared for.

"That's it, stay. I won't hurt you, see?" The girl reached forward slowly. "I want to help you."

She kept talking to him, softly. He liked the sound of her. But then she leaned forward a little too quickly, and he retreated again, half limping, half shuffling. He didn't want anyone touching him, or trying to pick him up, just in case there was another van close by. He had already seen one truck in the forest.

The girl came closer still. His paw was so tender, he wasn't sure if he could defend himself, and at this moment, he wasn't sure what she might do next. He tried to run, folding his bad paw beneath his chest.

"Don't! Don't leave! Please . . ."

Her voice got louder. Rumpus didn't like it. Once he figured out how to shift his weight, he could move more quickly, and he kept running. Within a few minutes, the girl was no longer behind him.

In time, he traced his way back to the clearing. The old oak was the only place he had found that could offer shelter and a place to hide. When he got there, the sun was high overhead, and the ground glistened with warmed-up snow. He sniffed the air. He was alone, at least for now.

Climbing lame was not easy. On his first try, he managed to grip hold of the bark with his good front paw, but he was not strong enough to pull himself all the way up. He tried a couple of times, then switched tactics, climbing one of the thick branches that hung low to the ground, his tail working hard to keep things steady.

Once inside, the darkness and cover of the thick bark walls reassured him. He relaxed a little and got to work on the bandage once more, tearing at the edges with his teeth. It came loose quickly, and he shook it off. The trap had left a semicircle of gashes on both sides of his swollen paw. They were deep. Deep and dirty. Gently, he licked himself, doing his best to clean out the grit and flakes of rust. When he could do no more, he laid his head against the soft bark of the old tree and closed his eyes.

Rumpus woke to the strange sound of something small and hard clattering and tumbling downward, knocking against the side of the old oak. He hoped it would stop and go away. His instinct was to lie low. But there it was again, a kerplunking-tippling-toppling sound.

Slowly . . . very slowly, he raised his head so that his gray-blue eyes could peer over the rim of the hollow. He did not see anything or anyone. But instantly he smelled something. His nostrils flared. Meat? No, not meatballs, something else. He raised his head a little higher. Then he caught sight of the girl. She was slowly walking toward the tree, carrying a plate with some kind of prey on it. Gently she placed the plate on the ground and backed away.

Rumpus sniffed the air again. He was not sure if he should leave the cover and comfort of the hollow, but he was hungry. And it was right there.

He climbed out and retraced his steps along the low-hanging limb of the tree, trying not to put any weight on his bad paw. His tail jerked as he tried hard to maintain his balance. He limped over toward the plate and sniffed. The pheasant was dead. He glanced at the girl. She was sitting cross-legged on the other side of the clearing with her hands in her lap, wearing the same red bobble hat.

Rumpus turned back to the pheasant. He chewed and cracked apart the bones, pulling off as much of the meat as he could and spitting out the feathers. It tasted good—not as good as meatballs, but better than hunger.

# Chapter 17

Maggie threw a second pebble at the trunk of the old oak. The cat's bloodied prints had been easy to track, but maybe he wasn't in there anymore. Maybe he had moved on while she'd gone back to the house, looking for something to feed him. She was about to throw a third pebble when a pair of small black-tipped ears appeared, just above the rim of the hollow. Then the back of his head. She felt her heart spin, a Catherine wheel whorl, alive with the glitter and spark of both fear and excitement. Every nerve cell, imprinted with the map of evolution, tingled with recognition. This creature was beautiful and magnificent but also dangerous.

She placed the dead pheasant on the ground and backed away. It had been hanging in Fred's larder. She had hated the feel of the feathers in her hands, cold and smooth, but couldn't think what else to give him.

Cautiously, the cat crawled out of the hollow. Maggie held her breath, mesmerized by his every move. Nothing made sense. He was obviously not a normal cat. He was far too big, and his fur was thicker and fluffier, and silvery. Plus his tail was unlike anything she'd ever seen. It was so long compared to the rest of him. And his paws were enormous. In a way, he didn't seem to have grown into his full body yet. Parts of him appeared too big for him to handle, but others were almost kittenish. Something about him seemed not domesticated, but not fully wild either. He was definitely not a cheetah. Cheetahs were skinny and yellow, and he wasn't the right color for a leopard. But that's what he looked like, a smallish silver-gray leopard. She didn't know exactly what he was or how he had ended up *here,* in a forest in Cornwall. None of it made sense.

Bones snapped and cracked as he ripped into the pheasant, making a mess of it within seconds. Purplish flesh and feathers scattered all over the place. She wondered where on earth she would find another dead bird. She vaguely remembered Fred saying something about finding it on the side of the road but wasn't sure. The cat licked the corners of his mouth. Then he glanced at her, and they made eye contact. The skin along her forearms prickled. Something about the way he looked at her made her think he wanted to trust her but couldn't quite bring himself to do so. His eyes were full of words unspoken . . . words unspeakable. Then he looked away, scanning the clearing as if he might run at any second. He seemed confused, she thought. And lost. But he didn't run.

Maggie stayed still, sitting cross-legged with her hands in her lap. He had been startled earlier when she had reached forward, and she didn't want to risk scaring him off again. So she sat on the cold, hard-packed ground, not making any sudden movements. Just watching.

The cat circled the base of the tree and picked a spot to lie down. He curled his body into a space between the thick, knotted roots of the old oak. Maggie could tell that while he was not looking at her directly, he was watching her just as closely as she was watching him. His eyes did not close but drifted into a half-hooded doze. Occasionally his silvery tail would flick from side to side until he seemed to settle a bit more and wrapped the length of it around his body, like a warm scarf. He yawned.

Maggie stared at his bright white teeth, at the finely pointed canines. A shot of fear darted through the pit of her stomach. She knew she ought to be more afraid than she was, and she did feel afraid, but more than anything she felt the awe of him. He was, in every way, spectacular.

She continued to sit until the light of the afternoon began to fade, until the end of her nose was pink and the tips of her fingers hurt with cold. She sat until he eventually got up, stretched, and limped back into the hollowing, his movements slow and silent.

Maggie stood up, her knees and legs stiff from sitting for so long. She felt pins and needles grip hold of one foot. In shaking it out, she kept her eyes on the tree. Part of her wanted to leave, to go back to the warmth of the cottage and find Fred. But the other part of her wanted to stay and sleep here so as not to miss a moment with him.

"I'll come again tomorrow," she said quietly. "Please, be here when I come back." Then she turned and reluctantly walked away.

A gust of wind shook the branches above. Maggie left the clearing, pausing to glance up. The sun had just set, draining all remaining wisps of color from the wintry sky above. The trees wavered. Time seemed to stop for a moment, suspended upon a different kind of axis.

She wondered if she had heard something, felt something, a whisper, not so much a voice but a strange kind of vibration. No. She shook her head and moved on, pulling her bobble hat down over her ears. Fred would be home soon, and she was desperate to tell him everything.

Maggie had just stepped inside the back door when she paused. Had she left the door ajar like that? She didn't think so. She knew better than to leave the door open in cold like this. The house seemed dark and quiet, eerie. Something stopped her from taking off her boots. She held her breath for a moment.

Somebody was in the house.

A burst of adrenaline raced through her. She had often had nightmares of being in danger and trying to scream for help, but no scream would come out. She could hear noises now. Coming softly from somewhere in the sitting room? Kitchen? They were not normal noises. Maggie put her ear to the wall. It sounded like somebody riffling through things, papers. She didn't know whether to try screaming or not. Would that scare them off, or would they come after her?

Maggie turned around and went back outside.

She crept to the front of the house, hoping that Fred's Land Rover would be in the driveway. It wasn't. She crouched behind one of the stone walls that encircled the front garden, but it was too dark to see into any of the windows. She would have to get closer.

She edged toward the flower bed below the sitting room windows. Some of the snow had melted, but most of the rosebushes were still covered and prickly. Squeezing between them was not easy. Slowly, she peered over the windowsill. The glass felt icy cold against her nose as she pressed forward, cupping her mittens around her eyes.

A man. She could see him now, bent over Fred's desk holding a flashlight. Short with big shoulders. Then a sudden blast of light as he turned and looked straight at her. Maggie ducked.

She heard a loud crash and footsteps thudding. He must have seen her. He was coming. Maggie turned and ran. Her boots hit the slippery gravel as she raced down the driveway, sliding and skidding over the ice, faster than she had ever run, her legs and arms pumping. She didn't stop to look back until she reached the gate. All she saw was the dim outline of the man now running toward her. She didn't wait for him to get any closer. She whipped around and ran onto the lane.

Maggie was still running when a pair of headlights bounced around the corner. She felt her chest explode with relief. Fred leaned out the side of the Land Rover.

"Maggie! Maggie, is that you?" he called out. "What are you doing in the middle of the road?"

She clambered into the passenger seat and started pointing frantically toward the gate, her cheeks hot and flushed. No words would come.

"Maggie, are you okay? Are you hurt?"

She shook her head and started pointing again.

"You want me to drive down to the gate?"

She nodded vigorously. Fred continued driving. Maggie leaned forward, her hands on the dashboard, scouring the darkness. But the man was nowhere to be seen.

When they got to the house, she led Fred through the back door. She switched on all the lights as she went and made loud stamping noises with her feet. In the sitting room, she pored over his desk. It looked exactly as Fred had left it, no mess, nothing out of place. She spun round. His filing cabinets seemed fine too.

"What on earth is going on, Maggie?" said Fred, perplexed.

"B-b-b-bur_________." Her head jerked backward. "B-b." Block. She grabbed a pen in frustration. *Burglar,* she wrote. *A man was here. Going through your things.*

Fred leaned over and read her note. His expression switched from one of confusion to concern. He turned and got down on one knee to open the lowest drawer of the main filing cabinet. Muttering, he riffled through all of the folders. When he got to one labeled *Patient records—Rosemullion,* he paused and flipped it open. The folder was empty.

"I don't know if I can quite believe it, but I think I know exactly who was here," he said. Fred got up. He put one hand gently on Maggie's shoulder and gave her a squeeze. "Come on, Maggie, I think we could both use a drink."

# Chapter 18

Rumpus stayed inside the hollow. The evening grew dark and cold. He dreamt of Rosie. There she was, he could see her, almost at the top of the climbing pole. He sprang after her, but there wasn't enough room and they both fell, landing in a heap of paws and tails, playing and wrestling. She was trying to pin him down, but he got away, just in time. They were back at the department store, at the Pet Kingdom, but it wasn't the Pet Kingdom. And then she was gone, just like that.

He kept looking for her, but she was gone.

# Chapter 19

Maggie and Fred sat in the kitchen after a quick bowl of soup. He poured a cup of tea for her and added a dollop of golden honey. The tea tasted strange, of dried herbs and flowers. But she found it soothing, and the more she sipped, the more she liked it. Her heartbeat began to slow. Fred poured himself a large glass of Scotch.

"The manor house, here in the village, is owned by a man called Lord Foy," he said. "Foy also owns a lot of the land around here, including Wildoak Forest. He wants to clear it, couldn't care less about the trees," he added, an edge to his voice. "Thinks he's sitting on a gold mine—well, copper actually, same thing, I suppose."

"I-i-i-is he?"

"Yes, there's copper down there for sure." Fred took a sip of his scotch. He sighed. "The thing is, copper mining can make the people who own it rich, but the people who mine it ill. Very ill. The missing file was full of medical records of patients I've treated for many years, all affected by arsenic exposure from nearby mines. Some of them got better. Some didn't."

"But why steal it?"

"Since last year I've been trying to stop Foy from going ahead. Partly because of the effects I've seen on my patients firsthand, but partly to save the forest. I love that forest, Maggie. Wildoak is one of the last pieces of ancient woodland left in the whole of the South West. Some of those elm and beech trees are hundreds of years old, possibly more. There's a magnificent old oak down there that's almost a thousand years old. It's seen everything: the Romans, the Vikings, wars of all kinds, and it's still survived. There are tawny owls, sparrow hawks and nightingales, badgers, hedgehogs and wildflowers . . . orchids and foxgloves and all sorts of butterflies." Maggie watched Fred's face get more and more animated. "There's a butterfly called the large blue. As far as we know, only two or three colonies remain in the whole country. And one of them is right here, on the edge of Wildoak! Large blues are on the brink of *extinction,* Maggie." He tapped his fingers on the side of his glass. "Well," he added, "who cares if just one butterfly goes extinct?"

"I c—are, Fred," said Maggie. "I care."

He looked at her. His eyes were soft and creased.

"I know you do," he said.

Maggie cupped her hands around her mug. "So," she said. "How did you try and stop him?"

"Last year I put together a local committee. I talked about the dangers of mining, of what I'd seen firsthand. The records were proof of all that. He's been after me ever since. I just never imagined he would go this far."

"What do you m-mean 'after you'?"

"Well, at first he tried to bribe me, with some, er, very generous Christmas 'presents'—a day's shooting at a big estate in Scotland. Of course, I don't shoot. When he realized I wasn't what you might call 'grateful,' he tried a few other tactics . . . like telling the *Truro Gazette* my memory was 'going' and people were risking their lives by coming to see me because I'd likely prescribe the wrong medications! Things like that can be very damaging for a doctor, even though it's all rubbish." He shook his head.

"A-are you going to call the pol-l-l-lice?"

Fred was thoughtful for a moment. "You're the only witness," he said. "What proof do we have that my files were actually stolen, and it wasn't me who somehow lost them? Besides"—he sounded dejected—"the committee doesn't have any real legal power. Technically, it's Foy's land despite all the rights of way and public footpaths that run through it. At the end of the day, he can do what he wants."

"So—he's j-j-just going to c-cut it all down?" Maggie felt a twist of anger. And then worry. What would happen to the leopard? What would happen to the old oak? "But he can't!" she said.

Fred drained the last of his Scotch. The ice clinked against his glass. "He can," he said. "And I'm sure he will."

"F-F-Fred?" Maggie paused. She needed to tell him. "There's s-s-something else."

Fred looked tired.

"I found something today, caught in a horrible trap. I think it was a l-l-leopard."

"Wait, *what*? What sort of trap? And a *what* did you say?"

"I think it was a leop-p-p-p___ard. His paw was caught in one of those metal-toothed snap things. It was so horrible."

Fred looked confused, then shook his head. "What did you do? Was he okay?"

"I got it off. But his paw was c-c-c-c-ut, badly. Can I take you to him, tomorrow? Make sure he's all ri____ight?"

Fred rubbed his eyes. "Of course," he said. "We can go first thing if you like, but it'll have to be quick. I've got to be at work by nine tomorrow." He paused. "What kind of animal did you say it was?"

"A leopard," said Maggie.

He got up and took his glass over to the sink. "Couldn't have been a leopard, Maggie. Whatever else it was, couldn't have been a leopard."

"It was," she said. "He had spots and a long tail. And he was big too."

"Maggie, there's no way you found a leopard in Wildoak Forest. They don't live around here," he said gently. "Was probably a big old farm cat. But yes, show me tomorrow. And I'll get that trap out of there. Come on, it's past bedtime for both of us." He turned out the lights. "Good night, Maggie."

Maggie bit her lip. She needed him to believe her.

"Good night," she said. She would show him first thing, and then he'd understand.

The next morning, Maggie was already waiting by the back door, fully dressed in her coat, hat, and boots, when Fred appeared.

"Come on, then," he said, ruffling the bobble of her hat. "Let's go."

Her breath puffed into clouds as they walked quickly along the narrow, wooded path. Once they came close to the clearing, she slowed down.

"He was hiding," she whispered, "inside the trunk of that great b-b-b-big tree. If we're quiet, I'm sure he'll come out." They crouched at the edge of the clearing for several minutes and waited. Maggie stared at the rim of the hollow, sure the cat would appear, just as he had done the day before. They waited some more. She glanced at Fred. He gave her a quizzical look. Still nothing. Maggie put her finger to her lips and quietly approached the tree. Her boots pressed against the hard-packed snow.

She got up close and peered inside.

"But he was here," she said in disbelief, staring at the empty space.

"Maggie, I can't stay much longer. I need to get to work," said Fred.

"Ok-k-k-k-kay." Maggie looked over both shoulders. But the cat was nowhere to be seen. "Can I at least show you the trap, then?"

Fred looked at his watch and hesitated. "Five minutes," he said. "But then I really must go."

"I know . . . It's not far, I promise."

Maggie led them through the tangled brambles and dense brush, past the fallen tree with shaggy roots.

"L—ook! You see! I'm not l-l-l-l-lying." She pointed at the bloodstained snow and rusted trap. It lay exactly where she had left it, like a discarded, strange kind of frying pan. She shivered, remembering the way the cat's flesh had bulged and the sharpness of his pain.

Fred got down on his knees. "I can't believe it," he said, surprised. "It is an old gin trap. They're illegal, been illegal for a few years now, thank heavens." He turned it over carefully. "Cruel as hell. Goodness knows who could've left it out like this." He looked around and then noticed his shears lying to one side. Maggie followed his gaze.

"Oh, your cutters! I didn't need them in the end." Her voice trailed off. "S-s—sorry, Fred."

Fred stood up and brushed off his knees. "It's all right," he said. He picked up the shears and was quiet for a moment.

"I'm not angry, Maggie," he said. "Clearly, you rescued some poor soul, and I'm glad you did. Most likely it was a wild farm cat. Charlie Timbrill's farm is crawling with them, and he's not far from here. It was probably one of his. Let's hope he's made it back there."

Maggie thrust her hands into her pockets. "I know what I—I s-s-s-aw, Fred. I p—p-p-romise you. He was too big to be a f-f-f-f-______." She stopped, switching out the words. "A cat from Charlie Timbrill's house."

Fred laid his hand on her shoulder. He looked at her intently, his pale blue eyes watery in the cold air. "Maggie, *there are no leopards in Cornwall.* That's all there is to it. Now come along. Let's get this thing disposed of. I've got to get to work."

They walked back to the house in silence, Maggie

trailing slightly. Fred seemed so certain. She started to wonder if perhaps he was right. But something about the blue-gray color of the cat's eyes, his markings, his tail, the size of his paws, made her stop. No. She knew what she'd seen.

They got back, and Maggie poured herself some cereal in the kitchen. She didn't want to admit that she didn't feel good being alone after the break-in. At the same time, she wanted the space to think about the cat and maybe do some research.

"I've locked every door and window in the house," said Fred on his way out. "Okay?"

"Okay," said Maggie. "Besides, I've got lots to do. I don't want to get behind with my schoolwork and give F__________Father any excuses." Which was partly true. Fred nodded and waved goodbye.

Once she heard the pop and bang of his Land Rover pulling out of the drive, Maggie cleared her bowl and went into the sitting room. It was dim on such a gray day. She turned on a few of the lamps and went over to the wall of bookshelves behind Fred's desk. Books about nature, trees, and birds filled the packed shelves, along with others about aviation and lots about the Great War. Maggie paused for a moment, reminded of Fred's fight with Father. Hadn't they both been on the same side? How could they have fought for so long? But then she caught sight of some dusty Encyclopedia Britannicas and lost the thought. She knelt down and ran her fingers across the tattered black spines. "L-L-L," she murmured. She flipped through the pages alphabetically. "Here," she whispered. Her eyes scanned the following entry.

> *Leopard (*Panthera pardus*), also called panther, large cat closely related to the lion, tiger, and jaguar. The name leopard was originally given to the cat now called cheetah—the so-called hunting leopard—once thought to be a cross between the lion and the pard . . .*

Maggie read on eagerly. The cat's coat had not been yellowish, and the drawing did not quite match . . . The tail was different, skinnier. Other parts seemed right though . . . small, rounded ears, the shape of his head . . . But it wasn't a match. She kept reading.

> *The lion, tiger, and jaguar also belong to the genus* Panthera. *The snow leopard, leopard cat,*

*and clouded leopard, although called leopards, are distinct genera.*

"What's a 'distinct genera' and what's a 'snow leopard'?" Her heart beat a little quicker.

*Snow leopard, large long-haired Asian cat, classified as either* Panthera uncia *or* uncia. *Its soft coat, consisting of a dense undercoat and a thick outercoat, is pale grayish with dark rosettes and a dark streak along the spine. The underparts are uniformly cream colored. The snow leopard attains a length of about 7 meters, including the 3-foot-long tail.*

Pale gray fur! Three-foot-long tail! Maggie reread the entry twice to be sure, then shut the book with a defiant slam. *He was a snow leopard.*

Her stomach bubbled with conviction. She had *known* he wasn't a farm cat. Quickly, she replaced the encyclopedia and went to look in Fred's freezer box. She would try again, but this time with some more food.

The freezer box was new, and Fred was rather proud of it. Maggie pried open the lid. Among the containers of mashed potato and cottage pie, she found one labeled STEAK. Hunks of solid meat pressed against the glass sides. Not ideal, but worth a try.

Maggie tucked the container under one arm, grabbed her coat and boots, then hurried out the door. She was halfway along the forest trail when something unusual caught the corner of her eye. A glint of something bright and blue amid the snowy whites and earthy browns. She stopped to look more closely. Were those gems? *Turquoise gemstones?* She knelt down and sifted through a handful of sticks and damp, snowy leaves. The gems were glued to a kind of animal collar, ripped and frayed at the edges.

*"Rumpus,"* she whispered, touching the engraved tag. She smiled. "Your name is Rumpus."

# Chapter 20

Rumpus had limped through his first few days in the forest easily enough. The cold temperatures were no problem. He had slept comfortably inside the hollow of the old oak, but catching food had been tough. The squirrels had leapt easily out of reach, and the rabbits rarely stayed aboveground. His paw remained a painful hindrance, no matter how hard he attempted to crouch or creep in silence. Try as he might, he still had much to learn about a place that was very different from everything he had ever known at the Pet Kingdom.

On Tuesday morning, he had been on his way back to the hollow when he had smelled and heard the girl. A gray-haired man was with her. Wary, Rumpus had stayed hidden, observing them from a distance, until they had left again. Now she was back.

He watched from the branches of a nearby yew as she entered the clearing and put down a bowl, not far from the base of the old oak. Then she walked away and sat where she had been sitting the day before. Rumpus flicked the tip of his tail from side to side.

His nostrils flared. The smell was inviting. Meat, red meat. Meatballs at last? He slipped out of the tree and crept a little closer. The smell grew stronger. He wasn't sure whether or not to show himself but soon found it impossible to resist. The brush wavered and he limped forward.

He took one close sniff of the bowl, then ate the cold, hard hunks of steak hungrily, devouring each piece like a chewy ice cube. When he finished, he licked the bowl clean, until not a morsel remained.

The girl had remained in her spot, quiet. Always quiet. Rumpus studied her. The way she sat, the gentle set of her mouth, the shape of her shoulders, her gaze.

Slowly, he ventured toward her. The girl stayed absolutely still. He came a little closer, until he was near enough to sense her full being. He leaned in and sniffed the outer edges of her mittens. His whiskers fanned forward, the sides of his nostrils opened up, and he inhaled the scent of her before pulling back. She was shaking, nervous. He pulled back some more and circled her. She did not move.

He caught the scent of damp wool, soap, and human

skin. Once again, he experienced the stir of a distant memory, of a time before the Pet Kingdom when gentle hands had held him and fed him.

He circled back around and faced her. The girl's eyes were alive and bright, but soft. She would not harm him, he was sure of that now. He glanced around the clearing, licked the corner of his mouth, and limped right up to her. Then he lay down, close but not quite touching. His paw was throbbing, and the warmth of her nearby felt good. Softly, it started to snow.

Moments later, the girl took off one of her mittens and reached out a small, bare hand.

# Chapter 21

In equal parts stunned and terrified, Maggie reached out to touch him. Delicate flakes of white snow drifted through the air, resting on his silver-gray fur. Slowly . . . slowly she laid her bare palm against his thick, soft coat. His fur was fluffier and softer than anything she could imagine.

"It's nice to see you again, Rumpus," she whispered, her heart expanding.

She wanted to lean closer and take a look at his wounded paw but didn't dare do anything that might scare him away. So she sat there, encircled by the forest, snow tumbling from the sky, marveling at the extraordinary presence of him.

Rumpus relaxed. He stretched out his back legs, then yawned, screwing up the skin around his nose and curling back his pink tongue. Maggie stared at his teeth, white, curved, and sharp. Again she felt the flicker of something primal, a fear that lay buried within the mysteries of thousands of years' worth of human

DNA. This creature was a wild predator. And yet . . . she found herself not wanting to leave his side. Ever.

"I wonder where you came from," she said quietly. "How did you get here, to Wildoak? I've told Fred about you," she added. "But he doesn't believe me. He thinks you are a farm cat." She stared at Rumpus, who was now licking his good paw and hooking it over the side of his head, rubbing and flattening one ear in the process, washing his face. "I know you're not though." She paused. "You're a snow leopard."

She thought she might burst into a spontaneous bout of laughing, crying, and laughing some more. Snow leopard. The words were hard to believe.

Rumpus finished grooming himself and rolled onto his side. Then he batted his paw into the air, swiping at the falling snow. First one and then the other. His tail flicked. He batted his good paw again, swiping and scooping the cold air. Was he trying to play? Maggie laughed. He was playing! He wriggled and rolled to his other side. Then he cuffed her arm and tugged on her sleeve with his claws, taunting her, daring her. She teased him, pulling her arm away. But then his paw skidded, and she felt the sharp scrape of his claws. "Ouch!" she said, surprised. "Those are sharp." Lines of dark pink streaks appeared on her wrist. She continued to taunt him but slipped her mitten back on.

Suddenly, a burst of chatter erupted from the birds around them. Rumpus scrambled up, nostrils flaring and ears pricked. He scanned the wreath of trees that surrounded them.

Maggie froze.

What had she done?

Before she knew it, he was limping away.

And then he was gone.

"Rumpus?" She did not understand what had happened. But a few minutes later, she heard the rumble of an engine. A cold, new thought occurred to her: What would happen if somebody else saw him? What would they do to him? *He was a snow leopard.* Leopards didn't get to roam free in the countryside . . . Leopards got put in cages. Or worse.

For a moment, Maggie recalled the piercing gaze of the tiger she had seen at the zoo, the emotion in his eyes. Perhaps Rumpus had already been caged;

perhaps he had escaped from a zoo, or some kind of horrible circus. Either way, he wasn't safe. She got up quickly.

"Hide," she whispered urgently. "And stay hidden."

Maggie was still trying to finish her math by the time Fred came home. She had been working on the same problem for hours and had not yet completed it. Her thoughts kept circling back to Rumpus and she found it hard to concentrate on anything else.

"Hi, Maggie!" Fred said, taking off his jacket and dropping his bag. He smiled at her. "I definitely need a cup of tea. Would you like one?" He picked out a mug with robins on it.

"Hi, Fred," she said. "No thanks."

"Everything all right? You look a bit . . . flustered?"

"Yes. Everything is all right." She closed her books. There was no point trying to do any more. "I have a qu-qu-qu-estion for you."

"Fire away."

"I——if, if the cat is n-n-n-n-not a farm cat, but let's just say he really is a leopard of some k-k-k-kind, what might somebody do with him, if they fou-ou-ou-ou—found him, I mean?"

"Maggie, love . . ." Fred sighed. Then he turned on the tap and filled up the old silver kettle. "First of all, he *is* a farm cat," he said gently. "A very big, very wild, very furry farm cat. But second of all, if he wasn't—then Wildoak Forest would not be the right home for him. I'm not really sure what would happen." He pressed the lid on tight. "He'd be lucky if he ended up in a zoo, I suppose, depending on which one perhaps, but that's probably where he would have to go."

"R-r-r-r-ight," said Maggie. She felt her chest get tight.

Fred looked at her. "You sure you're okay?"

Maggie nodded. Her thoughts were crashing into one another. She didn't want Rumpus to get locked away. Nor did she want to admit that Fred was right about the forest being the wrong home for him.

"All right, then," he added, unconvinced. "By the way, your mother called me today. She wants you to know that all your pets are doing well." He dropped a teabag into his mug. "She's even had Willmington, no, Wellington, out of his box and in her lap. Or so she says."

Maggie pictured Wellington's small pink nose, the twitch of his whiskers, and felt the sudden pang of missing him. All of them.

The kettle started to whistle. "They all miss you, apparently. She was very happy to hear that you'd been outside so much though. And keeping up with your studies, of course."

"What about—" Maggie paused, "my f—f—faaaa__________." Block. Her head tipped back and started to jerk back and forth, back and forth. "Fa-Fa-Fa-Fa-Fa—" *Oh, Father, my father.* She stopped trying to say the word and waited until the spasm stopped. She felt light-headed, like she might faint.

Fred was quiet for a moment.

"We didn't talk much about your father," he said. "Although she mentioned they were about to look around an institution of some kind." Fred stopped. He seemed unsure of whether or not to finish whatever he was going to say. "Why don't you write to her?" he added. "Tell her what you've been up to? I'm sure she misses you. Goodness knows, I miss her."

Maggie opened her mouth and then closed it again, in silence. She had been so worried about Rumpus that she had almost forgotten about Granville. Her thoughts crowded in, and she felt the floor tip, as if she might slide sideways at any moment. She had been away for almost a week, and it was clear that her stutter had not changed. At all.

"Come on," said Fred. He studied her closely. She couldn't tell what he was thinking, but he looked at her with such kindness that she felt a little steadier. "Let's have a bite to eat, then I want to show you something. My pride and joy, my life's crowning achievement"—he took an exaggerated bow—"my very own, almost-finished, well, finished-ish, Wing-ed Wonder."

"O-k-kay," she murmured.

The afternoon light was long gone by the time they walked outside. It had stopped snowing, but the air was still sharp and cold. Maggie was grateful for the distraction. Fred swung open the heavy wooden door and picked his way through the boxes and heaps of scrap metal. "Mind you don't trip," he said. "It's this way, through here." Then he slid open a wide slatted panel along the far wall that Maggie hadn't noticed before. Behind the panel was a strip of long narrow space, a kind of hidden room. Something huge stood in the center, covered by a tarpaulin, made up of odd angles and inexplicable curves.

"Take hold of that side, Maggie. That's it, now pull it back. There we go."

Maggie's eyebrows shot up in surprise and delight.

The extraordinary contraption was not so much a flying car as a fantastic combination of three-wheeler van, old-fashioned wagon, and some kind of rocket. With patchwork silver wings.

Fred opened one of the wagon-section side doors and motioned for Maggie to get in.

"How about a spin?" he said, dangling a large silver key.

"Love to," she said, climbing in. When Fred had first mentioned a flying car, she had hardly believed him. But here it was, a mind-blowing mishmash of steel, leather, and polished wood. Maggie had never been on an airplane and only ever seen pictures of them in magazines. "Does it really fly?"

Fred smiled and put the key into the ignition. With a loud bang and fizz of sparks, an engine roared into life.

"It might," he laughed. "One day."

# Chapter 22

From high amid the branches of an old beech tree, Rumpus breathed in the fullness of the forest. The air was crisp and laced with the scent of fresh snow. He listened to rustlings, whistles, and creaks, with ears that twitched and swiveled. He watched and smelled, his senses constantly on alert. Then he caught a slight whiff of burning carbon, followed by the sound of a rumbling engine. A few minutes later, a truck with big wheels and an open back came bouncing down one of the rough-cut tracks, stopping not far from where he lay. He had seen the same vehicle a few days ago and recognized it immediately.

"I want you to get started as soon as possible," said a tall skinny man, stepping out and slamming the door. His narrow shoulders hunched forward. "The villagers are coming around. I've taken care of that ridiculous committee too, and whatever 'evidence' that mad doctor had squirreled away."

"Very good, Lord Foy. The crew can start on Monday. We're ready to go." A second man got out, carrying a long paper tube. His breath was cloudy in the cold air. He unrolled the map and spread it out on the hood of the truck. "We'll start on the southwest side of the forest and move across one acre at a time. Some parts of it will be easier to clear than others, but we're well prepared. We'll have the whole forest cleared by late spring, I should think."

"Very good. Now let's walk. I want to see exactly where you're going to break ground." The tall skinny man circled around to the back of the car and pulled out a large shotgun.

"Of course. But I, er, I don't think you'll need your gun, sir."

"I always need my gun."

The other man shook his head and laughed. Then they left, walking westward into the forest and disappearing beneath a cluster of snow-covered branches. Rumpus watched them go, his ears pricked forward, not moving until their voices had died away.

He sat up and sniffed the air. He looked down at the truck. It would be worth investigating, just in case they had left behind something edible. Jumping down from the tree, he landed awkwardly and winced. Pain in his paw radiated up his whole leg, shocking him into a moment of stillness. It was not improving. In fact, the pain was getting worse.

The truck smelled interesting. Some of the smells were familiar, some new, but all piqued his curiosity. He sniffed the tires first and then the open back. Gasoline, mud, chemicals, pesticides sharp and nasty—he scrunched up his face—cow manure, dog saliva, dried blood, and something else he wasn't sure of. And then, feathers. Pheasant feathers! He jumped awkwardly into the open back and started to explore the mix of scents a little more, peering under an old blanket, pushing aside a box of shotgun cartridges and some poles and wires. There had been pheasants, he could smell them, but they were no longer here. He was about to look inside the driver's cabin when he froze.

CRACK!

BANG-BANG.

CRACK!

The distant blast of gunfire ripped through the soft forest air.

Rumpus leapt down and limped along the edge of the rough-cut track. His paws skidded along the icy snowbank and his tail lashed from side to side. It was difficult to run lame, but as soon as he could, he clawed his way up a tall, strong ash.

Moments later, he heard the men returning, their footsteps clomping through the undergrowth, then the jangle of keys and spark of the car's engine. He waited and watched while the truck reversed and drove back up the track. A strangely familiar scent filled his nostrils. He lifted his head. The truck bounced past.

For a second, he caught sight of something, an animal slumped on one side. A black-and-white striped face. The badger. Her shoulder was red and bloodied.

# Chapter 23

*Friday 1 March, 1963*

*Dear Mum,*

*You were so right! Cornwall* is *a magical place. I didn't think I would, but I really like it. A lot. I bet you loved growing up here . . . building dens, picking blackberries, running barefoot in all the fields. I can't imagine what summer must be like. I love the woods so much and have been going down to Wildoak every day. And Fred is so kind, just as you promised. I bet you miss him the way I miss you. And I really miss you, so much. I look at the photograph you put in my bag every night, and it makes me feel closer to you. Where was that taken? It looks like we were by the sea somewhere. I wonder if it was near here? I wish Cornwall was closer to home and we could come back together. Can we do that one day? I miss Wellington, Flute, Charlotte, and the others too. Are they really okay? Thank you for taking care of them. (I hope you didn't mind too much that I sneaked Hurricane and Spitfire into my pocket.)*

*Fred took me into his workshop yesterday and showed me*

*his favorite invention. You never told me he was an inventor! He calls it his Winged Wonder—he pronounces it funny, wing-ed, he says. We took it out for "a spin" although I can't see it taking off like an airplane as he hopes it will. He wanted to drive us down the hill and seems to think it might fly with enough speed, but it was too icy and the wheels kept slipping. I got a bit scared we might crash, but we didn't.*

*Has the snow melted with you? It's starting to melt a bit here, but it's still freezing. I love going outside though. I've never been to a place like Wildoak before, except in books of course. It seems . . . magical to me. I can't really describe it all . . . There's a beautiful old tree with a hollow in its heart. I know it sounds silly, but I think it was talking to me . . . Fred tells me the landowner is about to cut down the whole forest so he can mine for copper. I can't bear to think of that happening. Fred has been trying to stop it but doesn't think he can.*

*How much longer will I stay here? Will you and Father come for a visit soon? I think Fred would love to see you. He misses you too, Mother. I know he does.*

*Write soon.*

*I love you so much,*

*Maggie*

On Friday evening, Maggie sat at Fred's desk, holding one of his fountain pens. She paused for a moment. Now that she knew Fred, she hated the idea of not seeing him. She thought again about the terrible row he'd had with Father and how hard it must've been for Mum, caught in the middle. Then an image of her father came to mind, reading the letter over her mother's shoulder. She could imagine him shaking his head and pulling the knot of his tie into place, straight and tight.

*If your stutter is not better by the end of your stay, you will go to Granville Place for proper treatments.*

Maggie swallowed hard, trying to push away the panic that took flight inside her stomach like a sack full of moths. She hastily added a PS—*You were right about the air. You can tell Father I'm getting much better, in fact my stutter has almost gone. Tell him not to worry about Granville Place. I won't need to go. Really, my voice is much, much better. Also, I am keeping up with my schoolwork every single day.*

Maggie folded the crisp sheet of blue note paper and slipped it into a matching envelope. She wrote her mother's name and their address. *Evelyn Stephens, 143 Methley Street, London.* The ink spooled easily onto the surface of the paper, soft and smooth.

If only words could slip out like that, she thought.

Maggie held on to the envelope for a moment. It wasn't true that she was getting better. She didn't want to admit it, but she didn't want to lie either. She forced the thought out of her mind but didn't feel any better. Not telling Mother about Rumpus was also a lie. But what would she do if she knew? She would only call Fred, and Fred would tell her he was a farm cat and not to worry about anything. But he wasn't a farm cat . . . he was a snow leopard and *snow leopards don't belong in a Cornish forest*. How long would she be able to keep him a secret? What would Fred do once he realized the truth? What *could* he do?

Maggie got up from the desk. She trusted Fred. If anyone could help figure out what to do, it would be Fred. She would try again to talk to him. But just as she was clearing away the stationery, she accidentally knocked over the inkwell. Ink spilled across the desk and splashed onto the envelope. "No!" she cried, brushing it off. Her smooth clear handwriting smudged immediately. Maggie blinked hard. Now it was a mess. Messy and impossible to understand. Just like her.

She mopped up the worst of it with a handkerchief

and went into the kitchen. Fred was sitting at the table, surrounded by drawings and charts of the Winged Wonder, muttering to himself.

"If the speed reaches . . . no . . . no, there's not enough thrust . . ."

"H-h-hi, Fred."

"Hi, Maggie." He looked up, peering over his half-moon glasses. "Have you finished your letter?"

She nodded. "B-b-but I've smudged the address by m-m-mmmm-mistake. Do you have another env-v-v-v-velope?" she asked, feeling her cheeks redden with embarrassment.

"Don't worry," he said, taking it from her and turning it over in his hands. "It's still readable. That's what really matters." He looked at her and paused. Then he took off his glasses. "You know, Maggie," he said gently, "*what* you write is more important than the way you write it." Then he handed it back to her. "But I'm not sure I've got any stamps. You can check the top-right-hand drawer of my desk, otherwise you'll have to go to the post office." He glanced at the clock on the wall. "It's a bit late now though. You could go Monday morning?"

"Oh," said Maggie. "Ok-ay." The thought of talking to a shopkeeper, or to any kind of stranger made her feel sick, but she didn't want to admit it. She tried to push away her thoughts. "Fred, there's something else . . ." She hesitated. Fred looked at her expectantly. "I really need to talk to you. Ag-g-g-g-g-ain."

"Fire away."

"About the ca-a-a-a-a-at."

The expression on his face faltered. "Oh, Maggie," he said. He got up from the table and walked over to the sink.

"He's not a w-w-w-w-wild farm cat, Fred. I've looked it up."

"Listen, I don't want to make you feel bad, Maggie. I really don't, but you are a city girl after all. There are simply no leopards in the English countryside. There just aren't."

"Fred, he's a *sn-sn-sn-sn-sn*_________*snow* leopard. I'm sure of it."

Fred turned off the tap and turned around. He looked as if he might start laughing. Maggie couldn't bear it. She felt her chest tighten.

"I'm not j-j-j-j-oking," she said.

"Sorry," said Fred, catching the pained look on her face. He left the kettle by the sink and came toward her. "You have to believe me though," he said, taking her face in his hands. "Snow leopards live in remote parts of China and Mongolia, not villages in Cornwall. He's a wild tabby from old Timbrill's farm. Tabbys are beautiful. They can have all sorts of unusual markings, spots and stripes, and I don't doubt he looks a bit like a leopard." He added more seriously, "Listen, I know you miss your animals. Your mother told me how much they mean to you. And it's not that I don't trust you, I do. But I've lived here all my life, love. I know Wildoak like the back of my own hand. You need to let this one go."

Maggie nodded. He wasn't listening. She felt the backs of her eyes burn and for a horrible moment thought she was going to cry.

# Chapter 24

Rumpus was struggling. His paw was getting worse. Much worse. The soft black pads were swollen and throbbing. Dark yellow pus seeped out of the deepest gash, no matter how hard he tried to keep it clean. It hurt to put any weight on it, and climbing in and out of the hollow was getting harder and harder.

As the afternoon waned, he limped slowly toward the stream. He was thirsty and the cold, dry air didn't help. He wasn't far from the edge of the forest when he stepped out of the brush and onto one of the forest tracks. He did not expect to see an elderly woman walking a small dog. She did not expect to see him. They locked eyes for a second, before she started screaming and the dog started barking.

Rumpus turned and hobbled back beneath the cover of the trees as quickly as he could. He did not stop moving until he had made it back to the old oak. His paw throbbed uncontrollably, and the pain gripped the full length of his leg and shoulder. The wind whined through the wood, and he felt the old branches above him sway from side to side. He did not understand what had happened or why the woman had screamed like that. There was still so much about this place that did not make sense. He turned to licking his paw. The effort of so much running was overwhelming. Something felt terribly wrong.

The moon rose, smothered in cloud and blurred at the edges. Night closed in on Wildoak Forest. Rumpus fell in and out of a restless, painful sleep.

# Chapter 25

On Monday morning, Maggie walked reluctantly toward the post office. She pulled her bobble hat over her ears and tried to keep her feet moving forward. Her stomach tightened with a jagged kind of anxiety, spiked and edgy like the shards of a broken glass. She didn't want to risk speaking to a stranger, but at the same time, she really wanted Mother to get her letter, to know that she missed her and couldn't wait to see her.

Head down, she carried on. The air was cold, and her breath plumed into long puffs of pale smoke. The Big Freeze was finally beginning to lift, but it was still bitterly cold. A soft rain mixed with a veil of mist, amounting to what Fred had warned would be a day of Cornish "mizzle"—mist and drizzle mixed together.

The post office was a small stone building with a pointed roof. Maggie put out her hand to open the door and hesitated, not sure if she could bear to actually go inside. She took hold of the handle but then let it go.

Maybe she should just go home and ask Fred to mail it later. Yes, why not? She was about to turn around but then thought of Mother's face and how happy it would make her to get the letter, how quickly she would tear it open and sit down to read it at the kitchen table. Maggie sighed, a long deep exhale. "Come on," she whispered. She gripped the handle once again. "Come on."

A small bell jangled as the door opened. The post office was dim and cluttered, the walls lined with dusty shelves of stationery supplies, papers, magazines, and racks of faded postcards. There was a narrow counter at the front, stacked on either side with glass jars of ha'penny sweets and chocolate bars.

"Good morning," said a woman behind the counter. She had short curly gray hair and ruddy cheeks.

Maggie nodded and smiled. She felt the cut of anticipation and her chest tightened. For a second, she wanted to turn around and run back out again.

"I would like a s-s-s-s-s-s-ssssssss—" She stopped. The word would not come out. *Oh, please,* she thought. *Please can I just say it?* Stamp. *I would like a stamp please, to*

*London.* The woman was staring now. Maggie felt a heat rise around the base of her neck, and she pulled at the buttons on her coat.

"I would like a s-s-s-s-s-s-s-sssssss—"

"Stamp?" said the woman, interrupting sharply. Her mouth had flattened into an awkward line. Maggie felt a jolt of embarrassment. She had encountered this same stare so many times—judgment, verdict, and sentence all rolled into one. She had to force her feet to stay rooted to the ground.

"You want a stamp?" the woman repeated.

Maggie nodded. She placed the blue envelope addressed to her mother on the counter and slid it over.

"To L-London, please," said Maggie.

The shopkeeper averted her gaze. "Ordinary post?" she asked.

"Y-Y-Y________Y—" Maggie tried to say "yes," but the word felt trapped, and no matter how hard she tried, she could not push it out.

*"Yes,"* said the woman, interrupting her again. "Right you are."

Maggie hated it when people cut her off, answering

for her. It made her feel worse. She turned away and pretended to be interested in the old postcards while the woman pulled out a sheet of perforated stamps from a drawer. At that moment, the doorbell jangled again and an elderly woman in a headscarf bustled in.

"Shush, Tinkers, shush!" she said, scolding the dachshund yapping at her feet.

"Morning, Sue. I'll be right with you," said the woman behind the counter.

"Hello, Cheryl! Oh, Cheryl, have you heard the news?" said Sue breathlessly. She went on talking, as if Maggie wasn't there. "Doris says she's seen a *monster*! Right here in Wildoak no less! A monster-cat with blue eyes and long teeth. Saw it last night, she says, at dusk, while she was out walking Reggie. Swears on her life!"

The woman behind the counter put Maggie's letter into a mail bag. "That's three shillings," she said to Maggie. Then she turned to Sue, "What *are* you on about? What monster?"

Maggie rummaged in her coat pockets for the money. Her hands were shaking. They were talking about Rumpus. She knew it. *A monster?* Her heart slugged against her rib cage, pounding and pounding.

Sue went on, "Doris came over this morning, for tea, you know she always comes round mine on Mondays. She sits down, picks up a chocolate biscuit, and barely takes a bite before she says to me she's feeling poorly. Says she needs a brandy. A brandy! At nine o'clock in the morning! She did look pale though. So, I got her a brandy—not Bernard's best, mind you—and then it all came out, said she'd seen a vicious beast down the wood. Said it was silver like, with pointed claws and a huge long tail, and it'd run right at her. Said she'd never seen anything like it! The fright nearly killed her! Imagine! And you know she's got a weak heart. Reggie went bananas apparently, barking and barking, nearly pulled her over. And you know Doris. Cheryl, she's not one to lie." The woman paused to take breath.

Maggie tossed three shilling coins onto the counter and ran out, the door jangling shut behind her. The cold air was a relief. But her heart was still thumping and she felt uncomfortably hot. Now that somebody had seen Rumpus, it would be only a matter of time before the whole village found out about him.

*And then what?*

She couldn't bear to think about it.

The mizzle had turned to freezing rain by the time Maggie made it back down to the forest. She laid out a meal for Rumpus, although this time it was chicken, and not much of it. Fred's supply of frozen meat was dwindling, and she was worried he might notice.

Rumpus appeared slowly, his head barely rising over the rim of the hollow. He sniffed the air, but for the first time since Maggie had been visiting, it took him a long time to climb down. His limp seemed more obvious. He didn't appear hungry either, eating only a few pieces of the chicken. Maggie called out to him. He came more readily, or perhaps it just seemed that way, but he was lying down beside her within moments.

Maggie couldn't resist taking off her mittens and stroking him again. The fur underneath his belly was lighter and creamier than the silver-gray of his back and tinged with flecks of pale gold. He was so warm and soft. She leaned forward and lowered herself all the way down so that she was curled around him on the forest floor. The cold and wet didn't bother her at all. This was the closest she had ever been to him. She laid one hand on the side of his rib cage and felt the rise and fall of his breath. He lay still. After a while, she sat up.

"Rumpus," she said softly. "Are you okay?" His breathing did seem quite fast now that she thought about it, although she wasn't really sure if that was normal or not. A sliver of fear rippled through the pit of her stomach. Something didn't feel quite right. Normally he would be playing, batting at her scarf or tumbling over and over. She edged sideways so that she could kneel next to his face.

His eyes were open. Slate blue. Far away. He looked at her, but his gaze seemed flat.

"What's wrong?" she repeated softly. She leaned in, so close that she could see the dark pink smudge of his nose, the black rim of his eyelashes, the tips of his white whiskers. "You can't tell me what's wrong," she whispered, "can you? Because you can't get the words out." She laid her small bare hand on his cheek. "You and me, Rumpus . . . we're the same like that."

A gust of wind swung through the bare bones of the

nearby trees. The old oak at the center of the clearing creaked and swayed. It *was* hard sometimes, Maggie thought, being human. Hard to be understood. Hard to love and be loved. Hard to say what you wanted to say.

"If I ever find my voice, Rumpus," she whispered, "I promise I will speak for you."

The tips of his nostrils flared. His breath sounded heavier now, more ragged. Maggie sat up slowly, not wanting to startle him. She reached toward his injured paw. Until now, she had not been able to check the wound; he had never stayed still enough. Tenderly she lifted his leg and turned it sideways. "Oh, Rumpus," she said, her voice catching. The jagged cuts left by the trap's teeth had ripped through his soft black pads. The gashes looked raw and angry, steeped in dark yellow pus and red to the bone.

Infections could be fatal if left untreated, she knew that, especially if rusted metal was involved. But she had no idea how to heal him or how quickly it might worsen. Even if she told Fred and he actually believed her, she was no longer sure what would happen next. Rumpus would get taken to a zoo *if he was lucky,* Fred had said as much. The woman in the post office had called him a *monster*. Others were sure to come after him. Hunters. And there was no way she could carry him like this. Besides, there was nowhere *to* carry him. But clearly, he needed help. Urgently.

*Now what?*

Maggie took off her socks and boots. She always felt more clearheaded without shoes. The startling cold stung her skin. But there was something electric about walking barefoot in the forest, the feel of sharp sticks and iced mud, the snap of frozen leaves and frosted earth that shocked her sense of touch. She walked over to the old oak and sat down among the ancient, buckled roots.

"Now what?" she said aloud, throwing each word into the air like a folded paper crane, hoping it might fly, hoping somebody or something might catch it and respond.

She sat there for a while, curling her toes around the icy, rough bark. Skin to skin. Hoping.

Nobody responded. Maggie did not hear a voice. She did not "hear" anything. But something else happened. Slowly, bit by bit, a kind of energy seeped into the soles of her feet, spreading and rising throughout her body, fanning outward and inward at the same time, filling and spilling from the tips of roots and veins alike. The branches of her spine and neck tingled. She felt the crown of her head rise with a sense of being that somehow connected her to the whole world outside her body. She was no longer separate from the forest. She was part of it. And in that instant, she understood something—not in the way that words carry messages, but in the way that instincts carry feeling and intuition carries meaning.

*The forest could help.*

Maggie squeezed her eyes shut. When she opened them again, everything seemed a little brighter. She stood up and walked back over to Rumpus. She knelt beside him for a few minutes, gently stroking his cheek.

"There's a way to treat your paw," she said. "I'm not sure exactly how yet, but I've got an idea."

Rumpus raised his head for a moment, then lay back down. "Come on," she urged. "You can't stay out in the open like this. It's not safe." She coaxed him up and led him slowly back to the hollow. He struggled onto one of the low-hanging branches and crawled inside. "Stay out of sight," Maggie whispered. "I'll be back soon." She looked down on him, curled up tight. He seemed small suddenly. And so out of place.

She thrust her boots back on, feet cold and dirty, bits of twigs and muddy leaves sticking to her feet, to the insides of her boots. She didn't care. In the pale morning light, she ran between the trees, back to the cottage. She needed answers, and she needed them quickly.

But as she ran, she did not notice the slight tremor beneath her feet, nor the ribbons of gray smoke that plumed into the air on the far side of the forest.

# Chapter 26

The girl's scent. Soft. Something else too. Acrid. Faint, but unmistakable. Machines maybe.

"Rumpus!"

He opened his eyes.

She was calling to him, walking closer now. He recognized the vibrations of her boots, of her particular footsteps. But he could not bring himself to sit up. She was close, so close. He turned his head a little and saw the tips of her small pink fingers grip the rim of the hollow. Then her head appeared, her brown eyes, gentle.

"Rumpus," she said. "I've been reading all morning. Fred has loads of books, about nature and forests and plants. There are plants right here in Wildoak that can help you, medicinal plants. It's amazing, this forest is amazing. I'm going to look for some now. I'll be back as soon as I can."

He didn't understand the words or sounds she made, but her voice was reassuring, her scent comforting. He laid his head back down, and she disappeared.

The infection was already making its way up his leg and spreading throughout his body. His temperature climbed dangerously high and higher still.

# Chapter 27

Maggie washed her muddy hands in the kitchen sink. She had spent the afternoon gathering a basket full of what appeared to be twigs, bits of bark, and worthless weeds. A copy of *The Forager's Guide to Medicinal Plants* lay open on the kitchen table. It was a huge book with over eight hundred pages of tiny black text and dry, scientific-looking illustrations. She rolled up her sleeves.

"Okay . . . I'm still not exactly sure what a *poultice* is," she said, addressing Hurricane and Spitfire. The snails were now permanently housed above Fred's spice rack and surveyed the kitchen with placid curiosity. "But I think it's our best hope," she added. "A poultice, that is. Which, as far as I can tell, is some kind of paste made of mashed-up plants." She looked closely at the first of the pages she had bookmarked.

"Plant-ago lanc-eo-lata," she read out, "a species of flowering plant in the plantain family . . . ribwort, narrowleaf, ribleaf, and lamb's tongue . . . okay . . . so . . . the leaves are traditionally used internally—as syrup or tea—but also externally—for treatment of disorders of the respiratory tract, skin, insect bites, and infections. *Infections* . . . yes, we definitely need some of this."

She turned to the basket and sifted through the contents, pulling out several stems with clusters of tiny dark greenish buds at the top. She stripped off as many of the leaves as she could and placed them in a bowl.

"Next. White dead nettle . . ." She skipped through several more pages. "Here we go. White dead nettle, not to be confused with the common stinging nettle . . . used as a medicinal herb for centuries and is believed to have astringent, anti . . . spasmodic, anti-inflammatory, and soothing properties. I have no idea what half of those words are, but 'soothing' sounds good and it's one of the few plants that's actually growing right now, so it'll have to do."

She pulled handfuls of the soft, heart-shaped leaves out of the basket and added them to the bowl of ribwort.

"Okay, last one, stickyweed, stickeljack . . . cleesomething." She skimmed her marked entries. "Yes! Cleavers. Cleavers are used to treat a variety of skin ailments, wounds, and burns . . . also used to make tea . . . believed to assist lymph nodes in cleaning out toxins. What is a lymph node?" Maggie read the full entry a couple of times and decided to try both—she would add some to the poultice and also make a tea for him.

She glanced at the clock. It was almost three. Fred would be home in an hour or two. This was all taking longer than she had hoped, and she wanted to get back to Rumpus before dark. Grabbing a handful of the cleavers, she started grinding everything together with the back of a heavy spoon, adding little bits of boiling water at a time. The leaves and stems and sticky cleaver balls did not break down easily at first, but with persistent mashing, she eventually managed a lumpy kind of paste. It smelled sharp and sweet and not very appetizing.

Then she worked steadily through all of the instructions, cutting an old dish cloth into strips and filling some of Fred's empty jam jars with the mixture. But there was still more she wanted to do. Part of the book was dedicated to tinctures, with a whole section on the invention of "chemically formed aspirin," from willow bark of all things. Maggie glanced at the clock again, then quickly turned back to the open book.

"I don't have time to make cleaver tea *and* the willow

tincture before Fred gets home," she murmured, her fingers skimming more pages. "Well, the bark will just have to boil for as long it can. It won't be as powerful as a tincture, but at least it'll be something." Rushing from one side of the kitchen to the other, she filled up two pans with hot water. Into one she put the chunk of bark she had cut from a weeping willow down by the stream, and into the other she dropped a handful of leftover cleaver stems. A strange smell filled the kitchen. After a while, the water with the willow bark turned into a pale red liquid, and the cleaver water turned greenish-yellow.

Maggie was searching for some more containers when she heard the grind of wheels on gravel. Fred was home. Early! Quickly she shoved as many of the jars as she could into an old basket and hid it under the table. The back door slammed.

"Hi, Maggie," said Fred, coming into the kitchen moments later. He put down his briefcase and looked around at the stacks of dirty pots, smeared bowls, open books, and plant remnants. Maggie wiped her hands on her trousers and smiled awkwardly.

"What on earth are you cooking?" he said. "It smells revolting." He smiled back, but he seemed tired and the smile did not quite reach his eyes.

Maggie felt a pang of guilt. She wiped her sweaty forehead with a forearm. The kitchen really was a mess.

"I th-th-th-thought I'd try some new t-t-t-t-ea," she said, wincing at the half-truth.

"Interesting," he said. "I could do with a cup myself." He took off his jacket and sighed.

"Is e-e-e-e-verything all right, Fred?"

Fred sat down.

"Actually . . . it's been a tough day, Maggie. One of my patients has taken a turn for the worse, and I've just found out that Foy's crew has begun clearing the forest. They started today apparently. It's all going ahead." He paused. "I knew it would probably happen soon. I just didn't realize it would be this soon. It breaks my heart, Maggie. Wildoak is not going to be around for much longer."

With a sickening jolt, Maggie thought about Rumpus curled up inside the old oak. What if the bull-dozers got to the tree and didn't know he was in there and just razed it to the ground? Or what if he had heard them coming and tried to climb out? And they saw him? "H-h-how long will it take?" she asked anxiously.

"It won't happen overnight, but I expect they'll be through in a few months."

"There must be something else we can do to st-st-st-stop him! Your patients? Surely if people knew, about the p-p-oisons, how ill . . ." Her voice trailed off. Fred was shaking his head.

"For starters, I don't have any copies of the records, Maggie. And besides, it's complicated. While many of our villagers don't know about the risks of opening a new mine, many of them do, and will take their chances. Mining brings in work. Jobs are hard to find in Cornwall. It's not like London, you know. Sometimes it can be hard to care about getting ill later on when you really need a paycheck right now, when it's hard just to keep food on the table."

Maggie swallowed hard.

"I've tried everything," he added. "I really have. At the end of the day, the land belongs to Lord Foy. As the law stands, he can do what he wants with it." Fred looked exhausted.

Maggie sat opposite him at the table. She twisted her hands together and looked down. Her fingernails were dirty and almost green. She did not know what to say.

# Chapter 28

Time passed in a haze for Rumpus. Hours bled between two dark days and two dark nights. His fever raged, and his body trembled, breaking into fits. He was not aware of the girl coming and going or the strange-smelling paste she brought with her. Every cell in his body was at war, fighting to survive.

# Chapter 29

Within just forty-eight hours, Maggie was almost at the end of the poultice mixture. She climbed down into the hollow awkwardly. It was a tight squeeze, and she was afraid of hurting him by accident.

By Thursday morning, she had applied multiple treatments. She held the poultice mixture in one hand and looked at him, curled up on his side, one paw outstretched, caked and matted with dried paste.

"Rumpus," she whispered. "Rumpus?"

He did not stir.

Maggie had hoped that today would be different, that the plants would have started working. She had wanted him to be sitting up, alert, moving around. But he did not look any better. Her own breathing felt tight.

She managed to apply the last of the paste and put the jar to one side. Understanding what was really going on seemed impossible. She could no longer see the open wounds. Maggie reached out to touch the tip of his nose. His skin felt dry and papery.

"Rumpus," she said, bringing the remains of the

cleaver tea up to his lips, "you have to drink this. Please, even if it's just a tiny bit." She had mixed in a little milk in the hopes he might take some. She pried open his lips and trickled a spoonful into his mouth. She tried again. Eventually, he swallowed.

"That's it," she whispered, feeling a flicker of relief. He swallowed again, but she could not tell if much, or anything at all, had gone down. She kept trickling in tiny amounts little by little.

His breathing sounded faint and shallow. Maggie could not stop the worry from running riot inside her chest, her heart. She looked up at the patches of gray sky above and for the first time admitted to herself that perhaps everything would not be okay. Perhaps he would not make it.

In the distance, she thought she heard the low rumble of an engine. Even if Rumpus did make it, they were running out of time. With each passing day, Foy's crew was moving slowly and steadily closer to the old oak.

# Chapter 30

Rumpus did not know the girl was sitting next to him nor how long she stayed. His eyes remained closed as he drifted in and out of consciousness. The plants she had crushed and treated him with were doing everything they were capable of doing. But whether he was going to live or die depended on the complex series of chemical reactions raging inside his body.

At the end of the third day, dusk fell, and slowly, the earth turned on its axis. The stars came out. Darkness wrapped up the forest. A deathwatch beetle burrowed into the soft skin of the old oak. A barn owl flitted between the trees, the beat of her wings soft and pale. As his body began to shake uncontrollably, Rumpus succumbed to the fury of his fever.

On Friday morning, the sun rose slowly and without color. A red squirrel peered into the hollow of the old oak. He made a string of loud chattering noises. Another squirrel joined him. Their two small faces stared down at Rumpus, perplexed.

Rumpus opened his eyes.

His fever had broken.

# Chapter 31

Maggie dipped a piece of toast into her boiled egg and ate in silence.

"What are you thinking about, Maggie?" Fred asked.

Maggie looked up, unaware she had been staring down at her plate for a while. He was sitting opposite her with a mug of fresh tea in his hands.

"W-W-Wildoak," she said, which was half true. She was thinking about the forest, but she was mainly thinking about Rumpus and hoping desperately that he had survived the night.

"I can't believe there's n-n-othing more we can do," she added.

Fred took a sip of his tea. She watched the fall of his brow. They were both quiet for a minute. Then Fred put down his mug and leaned forward. He reached across the table and took hold of her hand. His skin was rough and warm. "Listen to me," he said. "We do what we can, in our own small ways, and sometimes that's enough to make a difference. Not always, but sometimes. I really do believe that when lots of people, perhaps hundreds or even thousands of people do what *they* can, things really will change. Big things, like the law." He smiled gently. "We might not be able to save Wildoak, but that doesn't mean we give up altogether." He finished his tea and got up. "Now then, where did that stethoscope of mine get to?"

As Fred bustled around and got himself ready for work, Maggie glanced at the local paper lying by the back door. It was still folded over, but she could see part of the main headline: Monster or Make-Believe? Big Cat Spotted in Wil—

She grabbed it and felt the air catch in her lungs.

For a split second, she was filled with wanting to show Fred, to tell him not to go to work but to stay home and come with her to the clearing and see for himself, and *help*. But he was already halfway out the door.

"Goodbye, Maggie. I'll see you tonight. Thank heavens it's Friday."

"G-g-g-g-goodbye, Fred," she said, throwing the paper aside.

As soon as Maggie reached the clearing, she knew something had changed. It was eerily quiet. She ran over to the old oak and clambered up the side of the trunk.

Rumpus was gone.

Small tufts of fur remained in the heart of the hollow, alongside splashes of dried blood.

"Rumpus?" she shouted, looking from side to side, frantic. She jumped back down and started to run around the edge of the clearing, wrestling with what could've happened to him. "Rumpus!" she shouted again.

The early morning sun bored through the branches around her, casting planks of hard yellow light. Maggie kept running between the trees, zigzagging her way through the forest, calling out his name every few minutes. She paused to catch her breath and leaned forward, panting heavily. Suddenly she felt a hand take hold of her shoulder, gripping roughly.

The scream caught in her throat.

"Why aren't you in school?" said a man with a heavy dark beard and slit mouth.

Maggie tried to speak. Her heart thumped. She stared at him. He was dressed in loose, muddied jeans and an old coat. His teeth were crooked and stained.

"I-I-I-I-I____" Block. "___I a-a-a—a-aaaaaam."

Spasm. Maggie's head jolted, and her mouth locked into a silent O. She could not get any sounds out at all. It was as though her windpipe had been cut off by a wire cord, cinched tight. The air stopped. Her head kept jerking and her eyes kept blinking.

"What . . . on earth?" The man let go of her. "What the 'ell is wrong with you?"

Maggie turned and ran.

She ran as fast as she could, back through the forest, down the banks of the river, through the orchard, and back up to the cottage.

It took her a long time to calm down. She went into the kitchen and lifted Hurricane and Spitfire off the shelf. Then she carried the jar up to her bedroom and lay on her bed, clasping it to her chest. Her hands trembled, and her breath came in rushed, ragged gasps. Slowly, the panic softened.

Maggie closed her eyes.

The man with the beard had shocked her. She knew that plenty of other people walked in the wood and lots more took their dogs there, but she had never actually run into anyone. He had not seemed like a dog walker. Maybe he was a construction worker and Foy's crew were already closer than she had dared imagine. But he hadn't been dressed like a workman.

Then a horrible thought crossed her mind. What if *he* had found Rumpus? What if he was some kind of animal trapper or a hunter? What if *he* had been the one to leave out that gin trap in the first place, on purpose?

Maggie sat up. She had to go back and find Rumpus. She couldn't just abandon him. He might be trapped, hurt again . . . or . . . what if that man had found him inside the hollow, too weak to defend himself? He could've thrown him into a sack or a box. What if he hadn't survived the night and . . .

She couldn't bear to think about any of it. She would go back, even though the idea of running into that man turned her stomach upside down. Something about the way he'd looked at her was so awful, like she was contagious. A wave of shame colored her cheeks. But the more she thought about it, the more her sense of shame morphed into something else. Something fierce. Fierce and determined.

Maggie placed the jar of snails beside her bed. "I'm going to find Rumpus," she said firmly. "I have to find him."

# Chapter 32

Rumpus padded slowly through the forest, his movements an awkward mix of jerk and flow. His paw felt so much better, but he was still stiff and sore all over. The rising sun had not yet lit up the forest, and he loped through the half-light of early dawn. For the first time in days, he felt hungry. And thirsty, incredibly thirsty. His nostrils flared. Something smelled different. Wisps of gasoline drifted through the air, rubber, and cigarette smoke. He sniffed again and fanned out his whiskers. Despite the freshness of the breaking day and the improvement to his paw, a shiver of unease rippled through his body. The birds sounded jittery and edgy this morning. Something was going on. He just couldn't understand what.

He continued on, winding his way toward the stream when he noticed a strange new gap alongside one of the tracks he had come to know so well. The air smelled different, of sap and fresh-cut wood. Rumpus cautiously picked his way forward. A rough-hewn clearing opened up in front of him, with a line of huge yellow construction vehicles parked on one side. He stared at the metal-toothed scoops, the black rubber tracks and thick round wheels, unsure why the machines were there.

Rumpus took a step back.

Oil, humans, sap, exhaust. None of this smelled good. He turned away. Wherever he stepped, things lay fractured or crushed. Tree limbs, pathways, a fallen bird's nest in shreds. It did not feel right. A glimmer of light caught hold of a broken spiderweb, hanging from a branch above his cheek. He stared at the useless threads dangling in the breeze, then retreated farther.

Circling the outer edges of Wildoak, Rumpus headed out to the far western side of the stream. The water rushed and rolled, tumbled and gushed, swollen with melting snow. He took a long, refreshing drink, then left the forest for a while. He still felt hungry and decided to try exploring the village again. Wherever there were humans, there tended to be food.

The village of Rosemullion had yet to wake up as he arrived. Somebody somewhere opened a pair of curtains, a door closed softly, empty milk bottles clinked. Rumpus stayed in the shadows. He kept sniffing, following his nose until he came across something that smelled sweet and salty. Meat, maybe? Rubbish bins?

A few minutes later, he crossed the road and came to the front of a whitewashed building with a thatched roof. It smelled of alcohol and woodsmoke . . . and yes, food scraps. He went to the side of the pub, searching for the source of all the enticing smells. There he found a handful of empty picnic tables and a pair of huge, overflowing dustbins. One swift bat from his good paw and the bins toppled easily. Gobs of mashed potato, half-eaten sausage, and gristly bits of steak, dripping cartons of cream, and butter wrappers scattered across the ground. Rumpus sifted cautiously through the mess. Eventually, he found a hunk of raw bacon rind and licked his lips.

Moments later, a car pulled into the front car park. Rumpus heard a door slam and got up. Footsteps. The footsteps drew nearer. Too near. He dropped the bacon and ran, accidentally knocking the bin. It clattered and rattled. A short woman dressed in a thick wool coat appeared around the corner.

"Anybody there?" she called out. "Hello?" She clapped her hands.

Rumpus took cover behind a wall, crouching as low as he could.

"Oh my goodness, look at this mess! Something's been at the rubbish again."

The sun was up now, and the village was getting busier. Time to leave. He didn't like it, the cars, the noises, the humans. He returned to the high street and crossed the road again, moving as swiftly as he could.

"ARGgghhhh! Wha— What is . . . *what is that*?"

The side door of a red postal van swung open, and a young man with thick glasses stared at Rumpus. Letters and parcels slipped out of his hands and fell in a heap all over the pavement. Rumpus hurried on. He was just passing the last of the village houses when a woman opened her door in a pair of slippers and a bright head-scarf. She held a small dachshund in her arms and was about to put him out when she caught sight of Rumpus. She dropped the dog and screamed.

"Bernard! GET DOWN HERE! BERNARD!" she shouted. "That's it! THE MONSTER, IT'S HERE, RIGHT HERE!"

Rumpus did not turn around. The motion of his

body was suspended for a split second as he registered the scream, and then he ran. He ran as fast as he could.

The sky was full and cloudy by the time he got back to the hollow. A light rain fell in tiny droplets, not quite freezing as it dripped and slid from the tips of bare branches. He paused at the edge of the clearing and sniffed the cold, glassy air.

Somebody new had been here. A man? Cigarette smoke, tar, sweat. And the girl. The girl had been back . . . the girl was still here?

Warily, he stepped forward, sniffing, searching. She sat in her spot, cross-legged in the rain. He ran toward her, knocking into her side and burying his head into the folds of her wet coat. He rubbed his cheeks against her body, again and again, chuffing and rubbing and chuffing some more.

"Rumpus!" she cried. "You're back!" She threw her arms around his neck. "And you're better? You're really better! What are you doing? Careful! Why are you doing that? Are you sneezing or snorting? Wait, are you *snorzing*?"

He could not tell if she was laughing or crying.

# Chapter 33

Maggie wiped her eyes with the back of her mittens.

"I can't believe it," she said in a whisper. "I was so worried. But look at you . . . your eyes are all bright, you're bounding around, *bounding*! Here, stop, let me look at your paw," she said, encouraging him to lie down. He rolled onto his back, tail flipping back and forth. He wriggled and swiped and latched on to her forearm, his claws tearing at her coat. "Careful!" she exclaimed. That hurt. His teeth were sharp as nails. She grabbed a stick and thrust it into his mouth, distracting him for a while until he settled down a bit. Then she took hold of his injured paw and gently inspected the wound. She let out a sigh of deep relief. While the fur was still stained with a messy combination of damp mud, green poultice, and old blood, the cuts themselves looked clean and sealed over. Two of his pads were a little swollen, but there was no sign of pus or redness.

She let go and playfully stroked and poked the sides of his belly. Instantly, he grabbed hold of her hand with all his paws and bit down on her arm. "Ouch! Rumpus, be gentle!" He didn't seem to know his own strength.

They played for a while, taunting each other, teasing, cuffing. Maggie sprinkled bits of dirt and leaves all over his belly. He swatted at them, whipping from side to side, ears pricked. Occasionally, a paw would land squarely on one part of her body or another and she would try not to yelp. She could hardly imagine how strong he would be once he was fully grown. She tried not to think about it, savoring the relief that he was back and he was better.

"Wait!" she said suddenly. "I almost forgot. I brought some leftover cottage pie for you." She took a bowl out of her bag and carried it toward the old oak. Rumpus leapt up and followed her eagerly. But he took one sniff of the cooked meat and looked at her with a kind of snooty disregard.

"It can't be that bad!" said Maggie, smiling. But when it was clear he wouldn't eat it, she gave up and put the pie back in her bag.

The sky darkened. "I ought to go now," she whispered. "It's getting late, and Fred will be home soon, if he isn't already." But she couldn't quite bear to leave

Rumpus, so she lingered, sitting down beneath the great branches of the gnarled old tree.

Rumpus chased a stray leaf in the breeze. He kept pouncing and missing as it danced in the air. He was carefree, playful. She looked over her shoulder uneasily. She had not seen the man with the beard again, but he would be back at some point, she was sure of it. And even if he wasn't, there'd be others. She thought of the woman in the post office and shivered. Rumpus had no idea he wasn't safe.

Maggie took off her mittens and touched the damp, cold roots. The bark was encrusted with iced lichen and felt rough beneath her palms. She closed her eyes for a moment and realized she was feeling it again, the same strange tingling sensation, soft, so soft, flowing through her, connecting her to something bigger than herself. Maggie felt linked to the old oak, to Rumpus, to the whole forest and everything that lay above and beyond it. The outlines of things didn't seem to matter. She was Maggie, Rumpus was Rumpus, and Wildoak was Wildoak; but she couldn't help feeling that something else bound all of them together, something infinite.

She opened her eyes. Silently, she said a kind of

thank-you, wondering if the tree could in some way understand her. The forest had helped save Rumpus's life, hiding him, holding him, healing him. She would never have guessed it possible, but as she looked at him now, still playing in the fading light of day, she felt the truth of it.

She stayed a moment longer, until the sun had set and the shadows were no more.

Fred was in the kitchen chopping onions when she got back.

"Hi, Maggie," he said, turning to smile at her. "You look freezing! Good for you for getting outside in such miserable weather."

"Hi, Fred. H-h-h-h-how are you?"

Fred tossed the onions into a large silver pot. "All right. Well, sort of all right."

"Did something happen?" Maggie asked, peeling off her hat and coat and coming to stand by the Aga. She placed her fingers against the warm oven door, allowing the heat to seep in.

"No, just that two of my patients wanted to know how my so-called memory issues were getting on." He muttered something about Lord Foy and grimaced. "Anyway, tell me all about your day."

"I-I-I _____." Block. "I-I-I tr-tr-tr-tr-tiiiied." Block. Maggie wanted to tell him about the relief of finding Rumpus, of his paw healing, of how she felt every time she sat among the roots of the old oak.

"I______" she blocked again.

Fred waited patiently for the block to pass. "You know what," he said, gently changing the subject. "It's the weekend, and I'm about to cook us a nice, hot dinner. You can help if you like." Fred rolled up his sleeves and headed out to the pantry. Maggie covered her face with her hands. She would have to find a way of talking to Fred sooner rather than later.

"Well, that's odd," he said, returning a few minutes later. "I thought I'd do a steak and mushroom pie, but I can't find any of the steak I packed a few weeks ago." He shook his head and murmured to himself. "Maybe I have got memory issues after all. I was sure I'd put several tubs in there . . . Well, chicken will do, or maybe I've got some leeks . . ." He turned abruptly and went back out.

Maggie stiffened. He was sure to find out now.

"Also, since tomorrow is Saturday," Fred said, coming back in with a bunch of skinny leeks in one hand, "what do you say we treat ourselves and go out for the day? It's going to be stormy tonight but clear tomorrow. I could take you over to the Helford if you like. There's a pub there with the best fish and chips in the whole of Cornwall. What do you think?"

Maggie's face pinched, and she felt her neck grow blotchy and red. She opened her mouth, but the words still did not come.

"I d——d——-d________."

"Or not," he continued. "We could go to the cinema instead. Have you ever been to the pictures? There's a cinema in Truro, and we could see what's on if you'd rather do that."

"Fred, I have to t-t-t——-t-t-t——" Maggie tried to push the words out, but it made no difference. Her throat kept catching, and now her head and neck were both jerking. "I have to-tell y—y——" She stopped. She would try tomorrow. When she'd had time to think more about what to say and how to say it. "Yes," she said, hesitating. At least it was the weekend and Foy's crew wouldn't be working on a Saturday. "Let's drive to the Helford, Fred. Let's do that."

Fred looked relieved. He turned to the sink and began washing the dirt off the leeks.

"Oh," he added, "a letter came for you. Looks like it's from your mother. I put it out, where, oh yes, there—on the kitchen table."

Maggie ran upstairs with the letter in her hands, grateful for an excuse to leave the kitchen.

# Chapter 34

Rumpus had watched as the girl left him, her red bobble hat darting between the trees. Then he had continued to bounce around the clearing, still full of play and mischief. With his ears flat and claws out, he pinned down leaves and trapped sticks. He sprang, jumped, and leapt, twisting his body in the air, delighted by what he could do now that he felt better.

In time he headed back into the arms of the old oak. Often, he slept inside the hollow, but sometimes he preferred to drape himself across one of the thicker branches. It felt freer that way, easier to run if necessary. He settled himself with one paw hanging down and his tail curled around his back legs. A cold wind ruffled his fur. For a while he lay that way, half-awake and half-asleep.

He was still dozing when the night sky clouded over and a storm gathered itself above the forest. Rumpus had never seen or heard thunder before. A sudden ear-splitting crack shocked him, and he jumped straight into the air, springing upward in alarm. The blaze of light and shuddering boom terrified him, and within seconds he had shot off the branch and was back inside the hollow, pressing himself as close to the ground as he could. Rumbles of thunder continued to roll across the surrounding countryside, hammering much of the snow.

Rumpus cowered inside the old oak and waited for the storm to pass. Somewhere close by, the earth opened up and a mighty old beech crashed to the ground with an ancient groan, snapping and tearing at the limbs of its neighbors. He felt the tree fall and sensed the ending of something.

In the morning, clusters of green-tipped shoots dared to press upward, piercing patches of snow and softening ice. Rumpus emerged from the hollow and sniffed the fresh air, flaring his nostrils. He was thirsty. He jumped down and headed out toward the stream.

The water ran fuller and faster than he had ever seen it flow. He drank deeply, then decided to explore one of the paths set high above the water's edge. He bounded onward, investigating new smells, curious about everything. In a short while, the path narrowed and dipped beneath the fronds of a large weeping willow. He crept inside the cove-like space beneath the tree's drooping branches. He sniffed: traces of human here. The girl? A small square of bark had been freshly cut away from the trunk, leaving behind a white patch, wet with seeping sap. Rumpus gave it a lick. It was tart and he screwed up his face. Then he turned and put his nose in the air, sniffing some more and pricking his ears, listening. Perhaps she had been here recently, but she wasn't here now.

Sunlight filtered in, and a strong breeze swayed the tree's long slim branches. Rumpus went back down to the water's edge. The stream was calmer here. Smooth clumps of brown grasses and pale rocks filled the riverbed amid the open patches of ice. He watched as a small shoal of fish sunned themselves, tails quivering. He crept a little closer, instinctively raising a paw. The tip of his tail curled up. Then a large, plump fish with a speckled golden-green belly and dashes of silver floated within reach.

*Whap!* Rumpus slapped his paw down and hooked the fish. It whipped and wiggled. Surprised, he flung it toward the bank, then pounced on it, water dripping from his chest and chin. He had never caught a live animal before and wasn't quite sure what to do next. The slickness of the scales, the texture of the flesh, the sharp spiky fin bits were bony and not at all like meat. And it kept wriggling! He poked at it, not sure whether or not this was a game. Eventually, it stopped moving, and he tried once more to eat it.

Abruptly he stopped. His nostrils twitched, and his ears flipped from side to side. Something was approaching. Musk? Male?

Rumpus listened and peered between the shimmering curtain of the willow's branches. There, on the other side of the bank trotting toward him, was a large fox. The tip of his tail was black and white, his fur a deep rusty red. Blood was smeared across his mouth.

Rumpus kept absolutely still. For a moment, the fox stopped, lifted his head and nose. Rumpus took a few steps backward. The moment passed. The fox put his head back down and slipped away, disappearing into the hedgerow.

It was mid-morning by the time Rumpus left the willow cove. He jogged back to the forest, this time passing a field of grazing sheep. He paused to stare at their black faces and at the small fluffy white lambs with pink noses. His instinct was to give chase, but then he smelled traces of the fox . . . and more blood. His gaze drifted across the field. Something had happened here. A killing.

Rumpus turned away. He did not want to encounter the fox again and besides, the girl might be at the clearing by now. Perhaps she would have food with her. Good food. Preferably non-scaly meatballs.

# Chapter 35

Maggie had not slept well. The storm had rattled every window in the house. She had dreamt of a hospital with stains dripping down the walls, of empty beds and leather straps hanging loose, and of children in identical robes, grass filling their mouths. When she woke on Saturday morning, her heart was beating fast and her cotton nightdress was damp with sweat.

The letter from her mother lay by her bed, propped up against the lamp. She sat up and read it again.

*Wednesday 6 March, 1963*

*My dearest Maggie,*

*I'm so happy to hear you are having a good time! We certainly miss you here, me especially. But you'll be glad to know I'm taking good care of everyone, just as I promised. Flute is loving his new perch on the kitchen windowsill. He chats to me now and loves sitting on my shoulder while I do the dishes. I'm not much of an expert, but I think his wing is fully healed. Wellington is quite mischievous, and though I can't yet bring myself to pick him up, I'm cleaning his box regularly and keeping him happy with bits of old cheese. He has grown quite plump. Charlotte is serene as ever. She seems perfectly content and looks down on me whenever I go into your cupboard to feed Wellington or check on the roly-poly boys. (Are they boys? How do you know?!)*

*Not much news to report other than we're all grateful for signs of spring at long last. I've started some work in the garden and am helping as always at the Salvation Army. I do miss you, my girl, my sweet, strong girl.*

*Father is well. Work has been a little slow at the office, but that was partly due to all the terrible weather. I've told him how much you are enjoying the countryside. I can't believe how slowly the time has passed. It seems like an age since I put you on the train. But not long now—we are planning to come down for a few days early next week. Father says he would like to see for himself how you are getting on. Will tell you more when I see you.*

*Better go here, I need to bring in the laundry. Looks like rain is on the way. Give my love to your grandfather but save most of it for yourself.*

*Mum xx*

*PS That picture was taken by the Helford River. It's one*

*of my favorite places in the world. See if Dad can take you one day.*

Maggie could almost hear the sound of her mother's reassuring voice wrapped into each word, but the idea of Father coming down to "see for himself" how she was getting on served only to remind her that nothing had changed. She had been in Cornwall for nearly two weeks now, and the truth was, her stutter was the same as it had always been. All the worries and fears she had left behind in London would still be there when she got back. She shivered at the fresh-cut memory of her nightmares. The specter of "treatments" at Granville loomed larger than ever.

"Maggie! Maggie, are you up?" Fred called out from downstairs. "The sun is out! Let's get moving. The Helford will be lovely on a crisp day like this."

Maggie put the letter back on her bedside table facedown and swung her legs out of bed. She wanted to see the Helford River and look for shells, but she was still worried about leaving Rumpus for a full day, even though it was a Saturday. It seemed as if a timer had just been flipped and the grains of sand were quickly slipping through. She could not hide here forever. Nor could Rumpus. "C-c-c-coming, Fred," she shouted down, her footsteps slow and heavy.

Helford Passage was a small village with whitewashed buildings perched on a steep, slanted hillside. Strings of little colored flags fluttered in the cold breeze, strung in zigzags from house to house. A telephone box stood on one corner, its red paint faded and peeling in the salty air.

"Here we are, Maggie. We'll park by the pub and walk over to Penwyth Cove first. My nan used to take me as a boy. It's where I first learned to find cowrie shells and where I taught your mother to find them too."

Maggie followed Fred along a steep narrow footpath, away from the empty car park. She had been quiet for most of the drive, and it felt good to get out of the car. They climbed over a stone stile and into a muddy field. At the top of the hill, Fred stopped and turned to look back.

"That's the mouth of the River Helford, see," he said, pointing over a hedge to a cluster of boats bobbing in the sea below. The slate-blue water was flanked on both sides by a quilt of rolling fields and hedgerows, a patchwork of browns and dark greens, covered in swathes of dwindling snow. Maggie gazed at all the little boats bobbing in the breeze. It looked exactly like the photograph.

"I don't remember, Fred, but I've been here before, haven't I?"

He turned and continued walking up the hill.

"Yes," he said over his shoulder. "A long time ago. When you were a toddler. You and your parents came down."

"Fred?"

"Yes," he called, striding on.

"W-wh-wh-wh-wh-what happened, with you and F-F-F____-Fa-Father? Why did you stop talking to each other?"

Maggie caught up quickly so she could walk beside him. Fred didn't say anything for a moment. He seemed to think about what he wanted to say.

"We didn't agree on something, Maggie. Something important to both of us in our own different ways." He glanced sideways at her. "Your father is not a bad man. But he's a damaged man. He tries to fix things, to control things, because he needs to find order in the world. He can't make sense of it otherwise."

"What do you mean? That's what you fought about? Controlling things?"

"No." Fred paused. "I know you've covered a lot of history at school, but your teachers, they can only tell you so much. The Great War was a terrible time. I saw things when I was a young man that nobody should ever have to see. And when I came home, I vowed never to take part in a war like that again. But your father, well, he came of age in the 1940s, when the Nazis were marching through Europe and the sun had yet to rise again. To be honest, we weren't sure it ever would."

Fred stopped and pointed out to sea.

"France is not too far from here, just the other side of the Channel. Hitler got pretty close to these very shores. We're talking twenty years ago now, which sounds long, but it isn't really. Anyway, I wouldn't enlist. Your father couldn't understand. Remember he's a lot younger than me, he was only a baby during the First World War, he hadn't seen what I had seen. So, he went ahead and joined up. That's what broke him. It broke so many"—he hesitated—"on the inside, Maggie. It broke him on the inside, and those are the wounds that doctors like me can't always heal."

Fred looked out toward the river mouth. Maggie

waited for him to go on, trying to imagine what it might have been like to fight in a war. Everything she had read or heard about it sounded so awful she couldn't believe it had actually happened. And yet huge gaps remained throughout the streets of London, town houses still in the process of being rebuilt, great craters of rubble where the bombs had fallen and destroyed everything.

"I became something known as a 'conscientious objector,'" Fred went on, "but your father thought I was a coward. He couldn't understand why I wouldn't serve, especially as I was a doctor. He still doesn't understand. In fact, that was the last time we talked, the last time you were here. We got into it one night and, well," Fred sighed. "It was best that we parted ways. But I'm not going to lie, it broke my heart, Maggie. Not seeing your mother for so long, or you."

Fred's shoulders slumped, and he turned to face her. For a moment, he looked old. She could see how much this had hurt him, and she found herself hurting too. She reached out her hand and slipped her small fingers into his. His palms were rough and calloused. She held on tight.

"You're seeing me now," she said.

Fred nodded. He squeezed her hand in return, and they kept walking, quiet for a while.

Maggie thought about Mother and how hard this must have been on her too, talking to Fred on the phone but not seeing him, not coming down here. Then she thought about Father, about the neatly polished medals in the glass container on his desk and the way he always placed his knife and fork just so when he had finished eating. She could smell the nip of starch on his perfectly ironed shirts and see the way he smoothed out his tie all the time. She thought of the distant look in his eyes when she had said goodbye, his body stiff and unyielding. He had never properly returned a hug.

"I t-t-try to love him," she said. "B-but he won't allow it."

"It's not his fault, Maggie."

The words from the forest echoed softly in the back of her mind. *It's hard to be human.*

Fred led them down the other side of the bluff, following the well-worn footpath, comfortable with every twist and turn. A small wooden sign with a crooked arrow pointed toward PENWYTH COVE and a flight of steep stone steps. Maggie had to take big, leaping strides all the way down. They reached the bottom, and Fred took off his boots and socks, rolling up his trouser legs. Maggie did the same. The fine pebbles felt ice cold and gravelly beneath the soles of her feet. She had never set foot on a stony beach before.

The tide was out, and shards of barnacle-coated rock protruded from the wet sand along the water's edge. She ran down to investigate, allowing the wind to loosen some of the heaviness in her chest. It helped, knowing why they had stopped talking, in some ways at least. But in other ways it only fueled her fear. What if Father decided to send her to Granville Place because that would be his way of controlling her stutter? What if he was like this because he'd been hurt on the inside and could never get better?

Maggie dipped her feet into the icy-clear water, allowing it to swirl and lap against her ankles. The cold shocked her skin.

"Found one! Here, Maggie," Fred called, holding something tiny between his thumb and forefinger in the air. "This is a cowrie. Come and see."

Maggie turned and ran back up the beach, her feet almost numb. Fred placed a tiny pinkish-peach-colored shell in the palm of her hand.

"It's b-b-beautiful," she said, holding it up to the tip of her nose and peering at it closely. The shell was no bigger than her fingernail. She turned it over, the underside creamy white and flat, its two edges folding into a narrow, toothed slit. It was exquisite.

"Now then, see if you can find one for yourself. You have to look really carefully, among all these pebbles. My record in one morning is thirty-seven. Let's see if we can beat it. I'll give you a shilling if we do."

Maggie thought of all the penny sweets she could buy with a shilling.

"D-deal," she said.

"Found one," said Fred a moment later, "and another. Oh, I've not lost my touch, no, I haven't. Still the best shell seeker in Cornwall, so I am." He laughed, his disheveled white hair ruffling in the wind.

Maggie looked and looked. She kept picking up what she thought was a cowrie only to find it was just another tiny pebble. She found other things though and soon filled her pockets with different kinds of treasures.

As the morning passed, Fred found twenty-nine cowries and Maggie found three. He encouraged her to lay out the contents of her pockets onto a wide, flat rock so they could identify everything: whelks, cockles, golden-yellow periwinkles, sea glass as smooth as her skin, and smoky-blue mussels with wide silvery mouths. The colors delighted her, purplish-pinks, pale green, bright yellow, cream, and gold.

"Pretty good for your first try," said Fred. "Hungry now?"

Maggie smiled and nodded. Then she scooped up all of the shells and put them back in her pocket.

The Captain's Arms was dark and warm inside. People filled the small, dimly lit rooms. Everything smelled of pipe smoke and ale. Fred picked the last empty table in a small nook by the bar. Maggie glanced at an old clock above the fireplace. It was half past one. She had loved the beach but was beginning to feel restless. Rumpus would probably be wondering why she hadn't come to see him yet. She hated to think of him looking out for her, waiting.

"What are you going to have, then, Maggie?" said Fred, putting on his glasses and holding out a menu.

Maggie considered ordering a steak-and-kidney pie just so she could keep half of it for Rumpus, but she couldn't quite face the idea of kidneys.

"The fish and chips are amazing. And they've got bangers and mash. Oh, I do love their onion gravy. Hmmmm, they've got mussels too, and pasties."

Maggie had still not decided when she overheard a snippet of the conversation from a larger table nearby.

"—Nigel Williams just lost two lambs last night! Guts ripped out an' all!"

"I saw them. Was not a dog that killed 'em. Torn to bits so they were. Mauled."

"Sue was telling me somebody spotted it in the wood. Huge thing, five-foot tail, green eyes, coming down Trewissick Lane."

"Didn't you hear? Sid the postman saw it *in the village just two days ago*."

Everyone gasped.

"Get Brae Thatcher down the woods with his gun. He'll take care of it."

"Maggie?" Fred tapped her on the head with his menu. "Can you hear me?"

Maggie swung round.

"Y-y-yes. S-s-s-s-ssorry."

"What would you like, then? I'm having the fish and chips. Can't resist."

"I'll have . . . the same."

Fred got up to place their order at the bar. Maggie leaned back on her chair, straining to hear more of the conversation. Two of her chair legs tipped off the ground.

"There's no time to waste. What'll it take next? Somebody's dog? *Somebody's child?*"

There was a stunned hush.

"A child? You think it might?"

"Maybe."

Maggie tipped her chair back a little more.

# Chapter 36

Rumpus spent most of his day dozing amid the branches of the old oak. Occasionally he got up to play, pouncing on unsuspecting beetles, swiping at shadows. He found a deserted nest and accidentally knocked it to the ground. He chased a shrew. He sharpened his claws. He napped some more, then he decided to mark the clearing. The forest was beginning to feel like territory, his own home territory.

Once in a while, he looked around for the girl. She still had not come, and he didn't know why. He carried on: napping, playing, exploring, stalking, snoozing, and lounging, until the sun went down and the day was almost over.

# Chapter 37

Maggie's chair could not tip back any farther. She held on to the table with her fingertips, ears straining.

"I think we need to call a village meeting. An emergency meeting."

"The longer we wait, the more likely a tragedy's going to happen. It doesn't bear thinking of."

"All right, leave it with me. I can talk to Mabel Harris and see if the village hall is free on Monday."

"Why not tomorrow, Dave? This is urgent, surely?"

"Agreed, we can't carry on knowing this thing is on the loose."

"And nobody works on a Sunday. More'll be able to make it."

"All right, let's see what Mabel says. We'll try for tomorrow, then."

*CRASH!*

Maggie's chair suddenly clattered backward, and she fell onto the flagstone floor.

A number of people from the table jumped up and came around to help her.

"Oh dear, you all right, m'love?"

"Did you hit your head?"

"Give me your hand, there we go, easy does it."

"I-I-I-I'm f-f-f-f—" Block. Maggie's head started to jolt and jerk. "F-f-f-f—" Her throat went into spasm. A few of the people stepped back, their faces perplexed, surprised and then wary.

"She all right? Does somebody need to call an ambulance?"

"She must've hit her head!"

At that moment, Maggie caught sight of Fred returning from the bar with a glass of lemonade and a pint of beer. Hastily he put down the drinks and reached for her.

"She's all right. There we go. Up you get. This is my granddaughter, Maggie. She's okay. Goodness, love. Your chair must've tipped over! Thanks, everyone." He picked up the chair and helped her sit down again. Maggie could feel the flaming color in her cheeks. She wanted to disappear.

"Hello there, Fred," said a man in a pair of jeans and a flannel shirt. He lowered his voice, but Maggie could still hear him. "Fred, she's not all right. I think she's hit her head bad. Couldn't speak right." Maggie lifted the menu and tried to sink lower into her chair.

"She's absolutely fine, thanks, Dave," said Fred calmly. "She's got a stutter, that's all. You carry on with your lunch," he said. "We're just fine." The man seemed unconvinced but returned to his table, where others were murmuring and whispering.

Maggie let out a long whistle of breath. Her cheeks were still flushed.

"You okay, Maggie?" Fred asked, sliding the glass of lemonade across the table.

She nodded and looked at Fred, but in the corner of her eye she could see that a few of the villagers were still staring at her.

"Don't mind them," said Fred quietly. "They should know better."

Maggie clenched her fists beneath the table. Her cheeks got redder. Making a fool of herself wasn't the problem; it was all the things they had been saying about Rumpus, about him being a terrible monster. It was knowing how vulnerable he was but not knowing what to do about it. It was the fact that bulldozers were clearing the forest, and all of those trees would soon be gone, even the old oak, though she knew, *she knew,* there was something ancient and special about it. It made her want to shout at everyone—at the villagers for being scared of Rumpus, at Lord Foy for not caring about Wildoak, and at Fred, for not believing her when she'd tried to tell him, for making her steal and tell lies.

A young woman brought over their food. "Here we are," she said brightly, "two fish and chips."

"Thanks," said Fred. "Looks lovely."

Maggie pushed her plate away.

They got home mid-afternoon. Fred opened the back door and hung up his car keys. "Maggie, what's wrong?" he said again. "You hardly touched your food, and you've been so quiet, ever since lunch."

He had asked three times now. Maggie nodded yet again.

"I'm f-f-f-f-f-ine. Really."

Fred was clearly disappointed. "All right," he said. "Maybe I'll go down to the shed, then, work on my car for a bit."

"Okay," she said sharply.

Maggie waited until Fred had gone out. She hated

to see him this way and couldn't bear to stay angry with him, but all she wanted was to get down to Wildoak and see Rumpus. She checked the kitchen clock. Three forty-five. She didn't dare take anything more out of the freezer but opted instead for a can of tinned spaghetti with meatballs. Slipping a can opener into her coat pocket, she headed out the back door. With any luck, the walk would help clear her head and maybe spark an idea. She hurried.

# Chapter 38

Rumpus sniffed the air. The girl! He galloped over to see her, blundering into her legs and rubbing his head against her knee. She stumbled sideways.

"Careful," she said, trying to catch her footing, "Stop! You're about to knock me over." She knelt down and put her arms around his neck. He chuffed and rubbed up against her shoulder and chuffed some more. He noticed that she wasn't as playful as usual. Something about the look in her eye was unsettling. She seemed . . . nervous. He kept rubbing his cheek up against her shoulder, but it didn't make a difference.

"I've brought you something," she said, pulling out the can in her pocket. "Oh dear, I forgot to bring a bowl though." She looked around. "I guess the ground will have to do. Come over here." She walked toward her spot and roughly scraped away a slushy handful of sticks and leaves. Then she opened the tin and emptied the contents into a cold, congealed heap.

Rumpus sniffed the clotted mixture suspiciously. He gave her a disdainful look.

"What's wrong?" Maggie said. "You were like this about the cottage pie . . . Do you not like cooked meat?" She sat down. Rumpus immediately started to paw at her. Surely, she would play now. But she didn't.

Something was wrong. He stared at her, and they were quiet, saying lots of things without saying anything at all.

# Chapter 39

Maggie stayed with Rumpus as long as she dared. The stars were out by the time she got back to the cottage, where Fred was in the kitchen, making soup. The whole house smelled of olive oil and rosemary. Maggie took off her boots and went to wash her hands. A pile of board games and some playing cards lay on the kitchen table.

"Hi," Fred said, turning around. "I wondered where you'd got to. Did you go down to Wildoak? Bit late, isn't it?"

Maggie nodded. She still felt angry and guilty all at the same time, but also scared. For Rumpus. She had not come up with any kind of plan. Time was running out.

"By the way, I put out a box there for you, for all your shells."

He had lined the box with cotton wool. Maggie ran over to Fred and spontaneously put her arms around his waist.

"Oh?" He seemed surprised. "What's this for?"

"Thank you," she said. "For today. I loved looking for shells with you. I will treasure them."

Fred put down his spoon. "Me too," he said, turning around and hugging her back. "Let's do it again sometime."

They spent the rest of the evening immersed in rounds of Scrabble and draughts, with Fred throwing his arms up every time Maggie beat him, which was often. For a short while, she tried not to think about Rumpus, the villagers, the forest, or what she could possibly do to stop any of it.

The next morning, Maggie woke to the sound of Fred's telephone ringing. He was still on it when she came down for breakfast. She had just poured herself a bowl of cereal when he came in from the study, looking concerned.

"Morning, Maggie," he said. "I've just had a phone call from Mabel Harris in the village. Apparently a group of Rosemullion residents have called an emergency meeting in the village hall. Noon today. She wouldn't give details but said it was a grave matter of public health and safety." He scratched the side of his head. "What on earth could that mean?"

Maggie felt the cereal stick to the back of her throat.

She tried to swallow without gagging. "C-c-c-c-an I come?" she asked.

"If you like." Fred took off his glasses and rubbed his eyes. "I wonder," he said, and then walked out again.

Maggie felt more nervous as the morning progressed and worse still as they pulled into the hall car park a couple of hours later. Cars filled every corner.

"Hop out for a minute," said Fred. "I'll have to park up the road a little way."

Maggie stood in front of an old stone building with a gray tiled roof. It reminded her of the schoolhouse at Southam Primary. And that reminded her of Nurse Nora, which only made her feel worse. Instinctively, she rubbed the inside of her left palm. The skin had fully sealed over since Fred had taken out the stitches, but it was still tender to the touch and the wound had left a taut, dark pink scar. Looking at it now, she wondered if it would ever go away.

"All right," said Fred, returning a moment later, "this way." The wind whipped his white hair to and fro. He opened a pair of heavy brown doors, and Maggie followed him closely. Several others came in just behind. It seemed to Maggie as if the whole village was turning up. She hoped nobody would recognize her as "the girl who fell off her chair and couldn't speak." She kept her head down, half wanting to take hold of Fred's hand, but she didn't.

The hall consisted of a large brown room with a modest stage at one end. Somebody had laid out rows of rickety foldaway chairs and put out a small table with large flasks of freshly brewed tea. The room smelled of floor polish and damp jackets. Most of the chairs were already filled with people talking and gesticulating to one another.

Fred and Maggie took a seat at the back. A few minutes later, a woman wearing chunky black glasses got onto the stage, carrying a clipboard. She clapped her hands to get everyone's attention, and the room fell quiet.

"Good morning, all, well, afternoon actually. I'd like to thank everybody for coming. As most of you know, my name is Mabel Harris and I'm the clerk to the Parish Council." She paused to clear her throat. "Now then, I want to get straight to the point. A number of you have raised concerns over recent sightings of a big cat in this area, a monster cat. It has also been reported that Sid

Curtis, our local postman, spotted the creature within the confines of Rosemullion village itself."

Maggie stole a glance at Fred. He was staring at Mabel Harris but turned to face Maggie, his brow furrowed.

"I saw it too!" A woman wearing purple gloves leapt from her seat and frantically waved one of her hands in the air.

"Yes, thank you, Doris." Mabel Harris nodded in her direction. "Please keep your seat. As I was about to say, so have other respected members of our community. But yesterday it was brought to the committee's attention that Nigel Williams lost two lambs in a brutal attack. He says they were *dismembered*." A murmur of surprise and dismay filled the air.

"I would like to invite anybody who wishes to speak up to the stage," she went on. "The Council will then decide how best to proceed."

The audience broke into animated chatter. Maggie's heart punched inside her chest. There was a rushing in her ears. Fred was looking at her strangely.

"Maggie?" he whispered. "Is there something you're not telling me? Has any of this got to do with the wild"—he hesitated—"*farm cat* you rescued?"

Her mouth and lips felt dry as sand. No words came. She kept looking straight ahead. Then she nodded, a small slow tip of her chin. Fred shifted in his chair and shook his head. "I don't believe this," he whispered.

Mabel Harris clapped her hands sternly.

"If you have suggestions or ideas, please, come up to the stage, introduce yourself, and share your thoughts openly, not among yourselves."

An older man in a cloth cap and beige sweater climbed the flight of stairs next to the stage. He shuffled on his feet and spoke quietly.

"I'm Nigel. Nigel Williams. I've never seen anything like what happened to my lambs. Their insides ripped out and legs torn off so they were, it was 'orrible. There's some kind of wild animal, nay, a monster loose in them woods, and I say we take care of it. Sooner than later." He stepped back. A small queue of people gathered along one side of the stage.

A woman in a bright headscarf got up next. Maggie recognized her as the woman she had seen in the post office several days ago, walking a dachshund.

"I agree with Nigel. We cannot delay. I think we should set a trap. If we don't, who's to say what animal gets taken next? My little Tinkers is tiny. He could never defend himself against a giant cat monster! Trap it. Trap it, I say."

"Quite," said the next person. "Lambs one day . . . beloved pets the next . . . and what about our little ones, toddlers? It doesn't bear thinking of. We must act."

A few more followed suit, until the last person in line, a man in heavy boots and a muddy jacket, got up. He had a thick dark beard and a wide slit mouth. Maggie felt her breath catch. It was the man who had caught hold of her shoulder in the forest.

"My name's Brae Thatcher. What's the point in trappin' it? Kill it, I say. Me and Ned'll do it. I 'ant missed a shot in forty years. Get some torches, a few beaters. We'll get 'im."

A shout went up.

"Kill him!"

"Shoot him!"

Maggie felt as if the room were tipping sideways. Her eyes smarted, and her throat felt tight. Suddenly, Fred got up. She watched as he headed purposefully to the front of the hall, shaking his head as if all of this was some kind of ridiculous nonsense. He walked straight onto the stage and waved his hands, commanding a fresh round of quiet. Maggie gripped the rim of her chair. She should be the one getting up, not Fred. She should be the one speaking out. Telling everyone the truth, that he was *not* a monster. He was Rumpus, he was a snow leopard, and he was lost. And none of this was his fault. How could it be? He simply needed help.

"I think most of you know me as Dr. Tremayne, or Fred." He cleared his throat. "I'd like to suggest we all take a step back for a moment. It seems to me that this whole business has been blown well out of proportion. I'm willing to bet this so-called monster is nothing other than an oversized farm cat. As always, the simplest solution is most likely to be the right one. This is Rosemullion Village, we're in Cornwall! There are no wild beasts, lions, tigers, leopards, or anything else in this village! Charlie Timbrill's farm is not too far from here, and I know for a fact he has a number of wild cats over there."

"But what about the lambs?" somebody interjected.

"I know what I saw with my own eyes!" shouted Doris. "Farm cats don't dismember animals!"

Fred continued, his voice calm but self-assured. "We all know that lambs get taken from time to time. It's only natural for foxes to hunt as needs be, or a dog gets out, and yes, often the results are distressing. As for 'knowing' what we've seen, it's well documented that our own eyes can be unreliable at the best of times, especially during moments of heightened fear or in poor light—such as dawn or dusk, which is when I believe this poor animal was spotted. I, for one, know there are times that I think I'm seeing things." He lifted his glasses up to his nose, and people laughed.

RAP-RAP-RAP.

The crowd hushed. A tall, thin man with hunched shoulders and a silver-knobbed cane made his way to the stage. He banged his cane on the floor as he walked.

"Thank you, Fred," he said. "I think we've heard enough from you. Ladies and gentlemen, I need no introduction, as you all know my family essentially founded this village generations ago." He then glanced dismissively at Fred. "You can step down, Fred. We all know you've been struggling with"—he tapped the side of his head—"health issues."

Maggie could see Fred was furious. So, this was

Lord Foy. He was thinner and more frail than she had imagined him. He lifted one hand to silence the room. "I, however, do not doubt the word, nor the eyes of a fellow villager. Whatever this creature is, doesn't matter. It's dangerous and doesn't belong here, call it what you will—monster, beast, big cat. The point is, our village, our pets, and, most importantly, *our children* are no longer safe. I have long believed Wildoak Forest to be a dark and dangerous place, full of pests and vicious creatures." Maggie covered her face with both hands. "But as many of you know, that's no longer something we need to worry about. For now, however"—he paused—"we have in our midst capable carpenters *and* capable marksmen. I suggest we do both—set a trap and send out a hunting party, without delay! We will not fail to protect our community." Foy waved and smiled a self-satisfied smile.

Loud applause broke out in the room.

Maggie felt hot all over, suffocatingly hot. The clapping air seemed thick and full of crashing waves, pressing up against her on all sides.

She could not remain silent. She would not.

# Chapter 40

As the village hall broke into applause, Rumpus was inching his way along one of the old oak's highest and thickest branches, very, very slowly. His ears were pricked, and his eyes were open. Wide open. He was stalking a small, shiny black beetle.

# Chapter 41

Maggie's legs trembled uncontrollably. Her tongue felt dry and rough. She stood up and walked unsteadily to the front of the room. She fixed her gaze on Fred, who was standing to one side of the stage. He was fuming. Lord Foy had stopped talking, and the hall was full of noise and chants. In the corner of her eye, she could see Mabel Harris clutching her clipboard, waving it about, trying to quiet the room. But everything looked and felt foamy, the sounds of things, the shapes of things. Maggie climbed the steps, catching the lip at the top so that she half stumbled onto the stage.

"Oh. Hello . . ." said Mabel Harris, arching her eyebrows. "And what's your name?" Then, turning back to face the room: "QUIET, PLEASE!"

Maggie stared at Mabel Harris, at her thick black glasses. Gradually, the background noise died down. Expectancy filled the silence.

"What's your name?" repeated Mabel Harris.

Maggie turned to face the crowd.

"Dear?" said Mabel Harris, a little more sternly.

"Please tell us your name and say whatever it is you want to say."

Maggie could see Fred, still standing to the side of the stage. He looked confused.

"MMMMMMMM——-—-M." She stopped. The hall was still. Somebody coughed. Maggie tried again. She felt the word rise in the back of her throat. Maggie, her name was Maggie. *Why was it always, always so hard to say?* But the air flow stopped short of carrying the syllables out into the world. All that came was a long, drawn-out "mmmmmmmmm" sound. She could feel the increasing panic spread through her veins.

"M__________MMMMMM__________" she tried again. Visions of classmates laughing at her, of teachers laughing, of strangers staring, judging, and pointing, crowded in on her. She looked down again. She thought of Rumpus, the promise she had made, that she would speak for him. *Try, try again.* "MmmmmmmMmmmmm—" She was afraid of blocking now, of jerking and shaking in front of all these people. *Please don't. Don't block. Just move on.*

She opened her mouth again. *Speak,* she urged

herself. *Speak, Maggie, and if you can't do it for yourself, do it for Rumpus.*

The very first sound to come out of her throat was a soft "H." A "huh" sound. It was the beginning of the word "He." It would have been the beginning of the sentence "He is not a monster." But within an instant, Maggie felt her mouth and neck block up. A second or two passed with her face unable to move, and then her head thrust itself backward and started to shake, her neck and shoulders going into spasm.

The sentence did not come out.

Mabel Harris didn't know what to do. She just stood there, gawping at Maggie. Most of the audience did the same. The expectant faces turned to embarrassed faces, and anticipation turned to awkwardness. Then one person let out a barely suppressed laugh. And others laughed too. Silly little laughs, thoughtless, hurtful, ignorant little laughs. But laughs just the same. Maggie heard them all.

The next thing she knew, Fred was by her side. He put his arm around her and led her off the stage and outside as quickly as he could. He helped her climb into the Land Rover and shut the door. She was crying now. She had let Rumpus down.

Fred got into the driver's seat and reached across, putting his arms around her, patiently waiting until she could breathe without coughing.

"Let's go home," he said gently. "I think I've got a lot of listening to do."

They sat at the kitchen table. Slowly, in her own way, in her own time, Maggie told him everything. From the beginning. How she had found Rumpus in the trap and rushed home to get bandages. How hard it had been to get the trap off, how hurt he had been, and how she'd tried to get Fred to come out in the days after, but then felt embarrassed and stupid when Rumpus hadn't appeared. She told him about finding the collar and discovering his name, about her guilt for taking meat from the larder without asking. She told how it had felt when Rumpus had first approached her, then played with her. That she'd felt *seen*. And how frightened she'd been when he got so terribly ill. But then the old oak had spoken to her, she was sure of it, and that was how she'd known to brew the herbs and make the pastes; the forest had helped. Finally, she shared her relief at finding Rumpus healed and how she had never felt so happy as when she was with him because, yes, he was wild, but he also understood. Because he was like her. He couldn't get the words out either.

Fred listened.

He did not once interrupt her, rush her, or finish off any of her sentences. He did not wince when she stuttered, and she did many, many times. He did not turn away or lose focus. He listened fully and wholeheartedly until she had nothing left to say and the light in the kitchen windows had begun to fade.

"I'm sorry for not hearing you the first time, Maggie," he said. His voice wavered. "I'm so sorry. Get your coat on, love. Can you take me to him now? It's almost dusk, and I fear we have little time."

# Chapter 42

Late on Sunday afternoon, Rumpus heard human voices in the distance. He was curled up inside the hollow of the old oak. The voices were not familiar. He lifted his head, hopeful the girl might be among them. She was not. He got up and lifted his nose above the jagged rim of the hollow so he could sniff the breeze properly. His tail flicked from side to side, hitting the insides of the ancient trunk. The voices made him uneasy. He climbed back down. The voices came and went. He fell into a light sleep.

A few hours passed, and by the time he woke, the sun had just set. Something was not right. The birds were agitated. The girl had not come all day. He waited. He waited a little more. Eventually, he climbed out, not sure exactly what he was suspicious of.

The forest was full of new smells he did not recognize. He stayed hidden in thick brush and moved slowly, watching, questioning. His senses were on high alert. Perhaps he ought to return to the hollow. But then he heard a rustle and faint snap. Close. Movement. He peered into the brush ahead, but he was upwind and could not smell or see anything. Then he heard them, humans, whispering to one another.

"We've got eight guns set up now, hideouts and everything. And the trap's ready. There's no way this thing is getting out of here alive, believe you me."

"Where'd they set it?"

"Down by the main ride, I reckon. Was the only place they could get the truck in. But we'll get 'im before they do."

Quickly, Rumpus slipped away.

Night fell swiftly, and the moon receded behind a thick, heavy cloud. Rumpus did not make it back to the old oak, deciding instead to get up off the ground and climb a young beech with solid limbs. He felt safer the higher he climbed. And there he stayed, ears pricked, peering into the darkness, watching, waiting.

At first, the banging was far away. But then it came closer, beating sounds, drumming, thumping. Rumpus didn't know what the noises were or why they were coming this way. Steadily they grew louder. He didn't like it. He could hear feet marching, a group approaching the forest. He sat up. They were coming down the main ride now, splitting up and fanning out. He heard shouting, whoops, and whistles, the smack and crack of sticks being pounded together. Now it was coming from all sides. His fur prickled; he paced anxiously along the branch. Then came the flaming torches, bobbing through the trees, balls of bright orange fire, close now, so close he could smell the smoke.

SMACK! BAM-BAM! SMACK!

"Whooooop! GET OUT!"

"GO ON! OUT YOU GET!"

One of the torches would be under the beech in a moment. Rumpus couldn't bear it anymore. In a panic, he leapt down and ran.

"THERE!" cried a man. "I JUST SAW 'IM!"

"GET HIM!" shouted another.

The men chased him through the darkness, shouting and yelling, torches blazing. Rumpus was fast but then more beaters appeared, spilling into the path ahead, all through the trees. Like ants, they were everywhere. He turned and turned and turned again.

"CLOSE IN, CLOSE IN!"

"HOLD STEADY!"

Rumpus kept running, now darting forward

between two crouched figures. He was fast. He got through. Now if he could only get to the edge of the forest. He ran and almost cleared the edge when a loud CRACK! BANG-BANG ripped through the air. The noise of the gun terrified him. He screeched to a halt and scrambled around without thinking. He ran back into the forest, blindly, swerving from side to side through the trees, doing all he could to avoid the clusters of orange fire that peppered the darkness.

He ended up on the only ride that did not seem to be filled with torches. He was running so fast that he did not see the shallow hole, nor sense the change in ground cover. But the ground fell away beneath his feet, and down he went, hard and fast, into a wide, roped net. It closed around him, tight. He tumbled and flailed, swiping and hissing, his claws thrashing out against the mesh as it lifted him into the air.

"WE'VE GOT HIM!"

Somebody fired two victory shots, and the cry went up around the wood. "WE'VE GOT HIM!"

A group of men dragged the net out of the ground, with Rumpus all the while lashing out, his limbs tangled up, teeth bared, still snarling and growling. They dragged his body off the ride and into the back of a large truck.

Seconds later, doors were slammed shut and Rumpus found himself netted and locked inside a thick wooden crate with two narrow holes. He continued to lash out furiously, thrashing and twisting his body, desperate to get out. But the more he fought, the more trapped he felt.

"Rumpus! RUMPUS! NO! STOP!"

He tried to turn his head sideways, straining to see through the slats. The girl. He could hear her voice, her feet, she was running, she was coming for him.

But now men were closing up the back of the truck, the crate was moving, he was moving, and she seemed farther and farther away.

# Chapter 43

"RUMPUS!" screamed Maggie. "RUMPUS! NO! STOP!" She could see taillights at the other end of the track, and the crowd, the torches. She ran faster.

"Maggie! Wait!" Fred shouted. She did not wait; she kept running, gulping air, her feet stumbling. But then she was on the ground, knees and palms slamming into the earth, mud in her fingernails, up her nose, tears. She was crying, scrambling to get back up. She had to keep running.

"L-l-l-l-let me g-g-g-g—go, F-Fred!"

"It's too late! Maggie!"

He held her back.

"No!" she shouted. "I have to go after him. What if he's hurt? What if they've shot him? I heard the guns!" Her words spilled out in a stream, choked only by a series of angry tears.

"Maggie, they're driving off. Stop!"

She beat her fists against his chest. "NO! Let me g-g-g-go, FRED!"

"Maggie! Listen to me! Maggie, I'm on your side."

She couldn't breathe. Her gasps and words mixed together in uncontrollable sobs. She beat her fists again and again, but he wouldn't let her go.

"Come on," he said eventually, "let's get you home."

It was almost ten when they got back. Maggie's face was muddy and tearstained, but her eyes were angry and bright.

"Wh-whe-where do you think they're taking him?" she said, flinging herself down at the kitchen table.

Fred took off his coat and hat. He turned on some lamps and lit a thick, stubby candle on the windowsill.

"There's only one farmer with a flatbed truck like that, and it's Nigel Williams. He's the one who spoke in the village hall today, about his lambs."

Maggie remembered the soft-spoken man in a cloth cap.

"They've probably taken him back to Nigel's farm. No doubt they'll lock the crate into his cattle barn, or some place with big strong doors." Fred came and sat beside her at the table. He ran his hands through his thin white hair. He looked tired.

"Where is the farm?" said Maggie. "We have to g-o after him. *Now.*"

"We can't go after him tonight, Maggie!" said Fred. "The authorities will have to get involved; the council, the police, there's all sorts of things that need to happen now."

"But, Fred! You said you would listen to me. Fred, please, h-h-h-h-ear me. Right here, right n-n-now! I need you to hear me *right here, right now*."

"I do, I did. But—" Fred stopped mid-sentence, as if he didn't believe what he was trying to say.

Maggie took in some hiccuping, shaky breaths. "When I first met you, Fred," she said, "you told me how much you l—loved animals. Tell me honestly, do you really think those men will keep him safe? If we can break him out of there, then at least we can be the ones to t-t-t-ake care of him. To come up with a plan."

Fred let out a long, deep sigh. The candle glowed behind him, flickering against the windowpane. "Maggie, surely you don't believe I can keep a snow leopard *here*, at the farmhouse?"

Somewhere, deep inside the back of her mind, Maggie did know this. She just didn't want to admit it. But she couldn't give up on Rumpus. Not now.

Fred looked at her. "I have my doubts. If it's left to that lot . . ." He paused. "In fact, that reminds me—"

He grabbed a pen and scrap of paper from one of the kitchen drawers, scribbling something. "Perhaps," he muttered. "Perhaps, Molly, oh, what was her surname? She might have some ideas . . ."

"I know you c-c-c-can't keep him here, Fred. But can't you at least keep him for now, until we can th-th-th-th-iiiiiink of something?" The insides of Maggie's stomach hurt. Her chest hurt. The backs of her eyes hurt. "And then I c-c-c-ould at least say g-g-g-g__________" Block. "Goodbye."

Fred sighed.

"Fred, please," said Maggie. "You are a doc-c-c-c-ctor. You know he's f-f-frightened and he might have even been sh-sh-sh-sh__________shot."

Maggie reached out her hands across the old pine table. "He c-c-can't get the words out," she said. "If I don't sp-speak for him now, who will?"

Fred nodded slowly. "Okay. I hear you, Maggie. So, what are you suggesting we do?"

"We go and get him."

"And then what? How could we keep him here . . . ? I don't have an enclosure or anything like that."

"You're an inventor, Fred. We can make one, together.

A pen." Maggie squeezed his hands. They were rough but warm.

"Make one? Now?"

She nodded.

Fred leaned back in his chair and laughed. "Okay . . . not impossible, I suppose. It's the 'go and get him' part that worries me."

"He'll come to me, Fred. I know he will."

"I don't doubt that, Maggie. But first we have to get to the farm, find him, and then get out again—which sounds simple, but if Brae Thatcher and his lot are there . . . I don't know if it would even be possible." He paused. "Besides, they put him in a crate. What if we can't get him out? How would we move the whole thing between us, let alone get it inside my Land Rover? There's no way a crate that size would fit."

*Focus, Maggie. Be practical. Think.* "We would need to cause some kind of distraction, something to get everyone's attention. It's a farm . . . we can do that," she said. But the crate. That was an obstacle she hadn't considered. "Wait, Fred . . . what if we don't ta—a-ke the Land Rover?" she said, smiling.

"What do you mean? What else is there?"

Maggie watched as Fred slowly grasped what she was thinking. His pale blue eyes glimmered.

"I know it's mad," she said. "But we have to try. I can't let him down again. I won't."

"All right," said Fred, shaking his head in disbelief. "We'll give it a shot. But we'll have to do it before the break of dawn, before they all wake up."

Maggie jumped out of her chair. "Come on, then! There's no time to lose."

For the next three hours, Fred's toolshed was filled with the sparks of metal cutting metal, the whir of his electric saw, the ping of nails popping out, and the slam of his hammer. Maggie worked alongside him, carefully. She measured and cut large pieces of heavy chicken wire, she sawed planks of wood, she stapled and nailed until her hands were blistered and sore. Bit by bit, she carried out pieces, and they assembled a large makeshift pen in the pale light of the moon.

"Okay, I think that'll do. Barely," said Fred, inspecting the hinges on the pen door with a torch.

Maggie shivered. They were outside by the vegetable garden, and the air was freezing. It was now close to one o'clock in the morning, and she felt a wave of tiredness wash over her. Fred stopped. "Why don't you lie down for a minute? This next bit is really up to me anyway."

"I'm ff—-fine," she said.

"You're going to need your energy if we have even the smallest chance of pulling this off, Maggie. Sleep for an hour. I'll wake you as soon as she's ready."

"Promise?"

"I promise."

Maggie looked at Fred in the dark, at the spark of protest in his eyes. She felt a huge wave of gratitude. "Okay," she whispered. "Th-thank you."

She went back inside the house, to the living room, where the fire had long since burned out, leaving only the glow of warm embers. She lay down on one of the old sofas and closed her eyes. But she couldn't sleep.

Where was Rumpus right now, this very second? Was he sleeping or was he awake and afraid, locked up in some strange crate? Was he hurt and bleeding? Did he know that she was coming for him?

# Chapter 44

"Who's a pretty boy, then?" A man with small eyes and breath that smelled of stale nicotine peered through the slats of the crate. He poked a long stick at Rumpus. He had been poking for hours. "What kind of wild cat are you? Eh? A cheetah?"

Rumpus hissed at him.

The man poked the stick in farther, jabbing Rumpus in the ribs. Rumpus swung round and swiped at the stick, growling. His paw struck, and the stick snapped in half, clattering to the ground. He had managed to wriggle out of the netting and was crouching as far from the crate door as he could get.

"Moody little sack of fur, aren't you? Go on, show us your teeth, then." The man picked up the split half, now jagged and quite sharp. He kept poking it at Rumpus.

"I'm tired, Brae. Leave him be. It's gone midnight."

"You kidding?"

Brae turned to a tall, skinny man sitting against the side of the barn. "Ned, this little kitty cat here shouldn't be alive right now. I only missed 'im down the wood because all them daft beaters was in the way. And I'll tell you another thing." He pulled a pack of cigarettes out of his jacket pocket. "People pay money for cat skin like that." He flipped a cigarette into the corner of his mouth and grinned. "Big money."

Ned shifted and leaned farther back against the barn wall. He yawned. A shotgun rested across his lap.

"Ned! Wake up and smell the roses!" said Brae. "What if . . . what if this furry fella accidentally 'escapes' from the crate? And come morning, you and I are here, scratching our heads, looking at Nigel telling him, *we don't know what happened*. One minute he was locked up, safe and sound, next minute he's gone."

"Brae, we're being paid right now to keep watch through the night. To stay awake so that doesn't happen."

"But what if we 'accidentally' fell asleep?"

"Both of us?"

"Yes, you idiot. Both of us."

"How would we not wake up if a wild cat was breaking out of a crate right next to us."

"All right, then, say we 'wake up." But it's too late, the beast is already running away."

Ned tapped his shotgun. "That's what this is for. You know I never miss neither."

"What is wrong with you?" snapped Brae. "What I'm saying is, let's shoot 'im and hide the body. Make it look like he escaped and then sell his skin for a tidy sum. I know people, Ned, in London. It's easy to flog stuff there. Nobody would ever know it was us."

Rumpus cowered against the far side of the crate. The voices, the smells, everything was disorienting and unfamiliar.

The men kept talking.

Rumpus was afraid.

# Chapter 45

"Maggie?" Fred gently shook her awake. "Maggie, we're ready," he whispered. He turned on a small lamp.

She opened her eyes and squinted at Fred. "I must have f-f-f-f-f-allen asleep after all," she said, sitting up and looking around at the living room. The events of the day flooded back. She threw off the blanket and jumped up. "What time is it?"

"Almost four a.m.," said Fred.

"Have we still got time?"

"I think so, if we hurry."

The night was piercing cold but silvery bright. Maggie followed Fred down to the toolshed. She glanced at the sky, at the net of bright stars and luminous moon. She was grateful for the light. They were going to need it.

"She's definitely big enough," said Fred, pulling both doors open, "I'm just not sure she's strong enough."

"Oh, Fred!" exclaimed Maggie. She stepped over two large dismantled wings, strips of metal, rocket boosters, and all sorts of machine pieces she couldn't name. "But your flying machine? You've broken it up! Completely."

Maggie's eyes traveled over the bizarre lumpy shape of what now appeared to be a newly minted half milk truck, half horse carriage with bits of wagon and spaceship thrown in.

"The engine is running great though," said Fred, leading her around to the back. "Which is the main thing. And look at this." He pulled a lever on the side of the rear, and a door fell down, creating a ramp. He pointed to a chain that was neatly coiled up in the back. "I'll be in the driver's seat, like we said, ready to go at a moment's notice. All you have to do is wind this handle, and that'll bring the ramp back up again." He pointed to a large crank that protruded from the mismatched floor. "See . . . and if we need to, we'll be able to get the whole crate in."

Maggie's heart was thumping inside her chest. She nodded. The whole thing was brilliant. Mad but brilliant.

"Right, warm enough?" said Fred. "It's cold out there."

She smiled. "Warm enough."

The flying machine no longer had wings, but Maggie wondered if it might actually take off. Her seat belt was literally a belt, one of Fred's, and did not seem at all sturdy. There were no doors up front, and she was sitting on a seat that looked like an old dentist's chair of some kind. The engine roared and popped and banged as they made it through the gate and down the lane.

"C-c-can we go over the p-p-plan one more time, Fred?"

Fred's hands gripped the steering wheel as if it might come off at any moment. Maggie tried not to look.

"Yes. I'm going to park just outside the farm gate. You slip down the driveway and into the farmyard. Then . . . first of all, find Rumpus. Next, cause a diversion, and then, when you're ready, give the signal for me to reverse down. Together we'll load him up as quick as we can and get out."

"What's the signal?"

"Look in the compartment by your knees. There's a sailing flare in there. Just aim it at the sky and pull the cord, see. Hang it round your neck for now. I'll be watching and will come straight down soon as I see it.

But the road is narrow, mind, so I might have to reverse in backward."

Maggie crossed her fingers. She was feeling less confident by the minute.

They continued on for several miles until they came to a lane with a hand-painted sign that said TREGURRALL FARM, above the silhouette of a cow. Fred turned and brought the flying machine as far along the lane as he dared. He stopped the engine. Then he motioned for Maggie to get out.

"For good luck," he whispered, leaning over and placing a small acorn in the palm of her hand. Maggie smiled at him. She slipped the acorn into her pocket and climbed out. Fred waved at her and then pointed down the hill toward the dim outline of several buildings clustered around an open courtyard.

Maggie stuck close to the verge. When she reached the bottom of the hill, she came to a large metal five-bar gate. She was about to climb over it when she realized Fred would need it open, especially if he was reversing. She pulled the bolt to one side and pushed the gate open. The large, rusted hinges squeaked. And squeaked again the more she pushed, a very loud squeak. Maggie froze for a moment, stopping the gate mid-swing. A dog started barking. Gritting her teeth, she quickly opened the gate all the way, wincing as it squeaked once more. She froze for a moment, heart thumping. Would somebody have heard the dog? She peered at the cluster of buildings, watching anxiously for a light to come on. None did, although it seemed to take forever for the dog to stop barking.

Still nervous, she continued along the uneven driveway until she reached the main yard. The air smelled like a farm, rich with horse manure and damp hay. She decided to check the buildings with big doors first, beginning with a large barn. The door on one side opened into a tack room laden with heavy leather saddles and all sorts of bridles and ropes and horse things. Then she ventured into a set of stables, slipping between the shadows silently. Two huge shire horses eyed her in the darkness with a soft-muzzled curiosity. Maggie half wanted to stop and pet them, they were so beautiful and gentle-looking, but she refrained. Rumpus was not there. He wasn't in any of the empty stables. The only thing she found was a stack of hay bales and sacks of horse feed. She left and ran quickly to a smaller barn next door. More empty stalls, a frightened rat, but no crate.

The light outside seemed to be building. Dawn could not be more than half an hour away. Maggie ran from one building to the next. Soon, she began to worry that Fred had been wrong, that perhaps this wasn't even the right farm. She checked every enclosure she could find from a large chicken coop to a metal pigpen. Still nothing.

She swung round, scanning all directions, but it was no use. She would have to go back and tell Fred they had made a terrible mistake. Maggie was on her way out when a small flicker of orange light caught the corner of her eye. She turned. Was that a shed? Had she been in there? She wasn't sure. The building was small and rickety and tucked behind the chicken coop. A second light flickered to life. It looked like the strike of a match. Then a dot of orange. Somebody was lighting a cigarette.

Maggie turned around and crept closer to the shed. She crouched beneath a small, grimy window and slowly raised her head above the ledge. Brae Thatcher stood at one end, in front of another man, tall and skinny. Maggie gasped. Brae had a gun, a long-barreled shotgun. They were having an argument; their voices carried through the air, angry and muffled. She stood on her tiptoes, straining to see more. Behind the two men she caught a glimpse of something, a crate . . . slatted bars. Rumpus!

Maggie felt a double gut punch of fear and anger. She had not expected these men to have guns.

Several things then happened in rapid, hectic succession. Brae Thatcher suddenly snatched the shotgun out of the skinny man's hands, and loaded it. He got down on his knees and pushed the barrel of the gun between the slats. Maggie grabbed hold of the flare around her neck and pulled out the pin. She fired it not at the sky as Fred had instructed, but at the side of the chicken coop next door. The flare hit hard, and a sudden burst of bright red light exploded across the farmyard with a loud *Bang!* Scores of panicked chickens erupted out of the coop, screeching and squawking, triggering a chain reaction amongst all of the animals.

Maggie hoped with all her heart that Fred might

have seen the red glow, even though it wasn't high in the sky. Either way, there was no time to find out. Their plan was already in tatters.

At that moment, the doors of the shed flung open and the two men ran out, Brae still holding the shotgun. Lights were turned on; dogs started barking, joining all the animals shrieking and howling in alarm. Maggie slipped inside the shed and ran over to the crate. She pressed her palms against the open slats at the back.

"Rumpus? Rumpus? Are you all right?" she whispered.

He thrust his head against the side of the crate, rubbing and chuffing at the sound of her voice.

"Oh, Rumpus! Thank goodness. You're okay," said Maggie, squeezing her hand inside. "I see you. I'm here. Yes, it's me, Maggie. Quick, we must be quick. I've got to get you out of here. Can I . . . ? How . . . ?" She ran her fingertips over the wooden door to the crate. Two main bolts were fastened, but both had been secured with a layer of thick knotted rope. Maggie's fingers trembled as she worked the tight twists. There was no way they'd be able to move the crate without being seen now, even if Fred was already on his way down with the crank. *Hurry, hurry.*

The noise outside was close to hysterical. Maggie could hear more people shouting and running, foot-steps, coming this way. *Come on!* At last the first knot came loose. She started on the second. Rumpus paced up and down inside, panting.

"I think I can get this . . . open," Maggie said, straining her fingers. "Oh, come on! But you have to follow me, Rumpus . . . There!" She got the second of the two knots untied, released the bolts, and flung open the door.

Rumpus was overjoyed to see her, nudging and pawing and pressing up against her. Maggie had to restrain herself from stopping to hug him. "We have to go, Rumpus! Quick, come!" she urged him. "Come on!" She scooped at the air, beckoning him, frantic. When he still didn't move, she crawled toward him on her hands and knees, until her head and shoulders were in the crate.

Suddenly, the noise from outside burst into the shed, footsteps, running, shouts.

"Rumpus, *now*!" Maggie reached for him.

"Hey! What's this?" The voice was angry.

Maggie felt her chest clamp, and for a second, she couldn't breathe. Brae Thatcher was now peering into the crate, blocking her only way out.

"What the hell are *you* doing in there?" he shouted, his face contorting with surprise and angry disbelief.

Maggie screamed. Then she felt his hand come down on her shoulder, yanking, and forcing her to a halt, his fingers pinching like a vise. She tried to wrest herself free, but his grip was too tight. Then she did the only thing she could think of to make him let go. She bit him. Hard. Brae let out a high-pitched yelp of pain and clutched his forearm.

"You little witch!" he yelled furiously. Maggie ran. "Rumpus!" she shouted. "This way!" For a moment, the snow leopard paused, his eyes taking in the chaos. Chickens were loose everywhere. Nigel and his wife were now in the yard, in their pajamas, chasing the chickens. Geese were honking, dogs still barking. Maggie stopped to look back, panicked that Rumpus would swerve and chase after the chickens or the geese. But he stayed with her.

"Stop her! Ned? NED! She's stealing the cat! MOVE IT!" yelled Brae. "Run, for heaven's sake, run!"

Maggie did not stop sprinting until she saw the clunky silhouette of the flying machine slowly reversing down the lane, a random assortment of lights blinking in the half-light. She ran up to it and banged on the back doors, before remembering the lever on the side. She pulled it down hard. The ramp lowered, and she clambered in. But Rumpus hesitated. In the emerging light of dawn, she could see the two men running fast up the hill. "Rumpus, come," she whispered, annoyed she had not thought to bring food for him. "Climb in here. It's okay." The men were getting closer. Rumpus's eyes flashed nervously. He paced from side to side, tail flicking. "Rumpus, please, just get in!" But still he paced.

Maggie climbed back out. She had never tried to pick him up before and didn't know how he would react, but she was desperate.

"Trust me," she whispered, "please, trust me."

"STOP! You're a thief, you are! STOP right there!"

Maggie did her best to scoop her arms around Rumpus. He was large and heavy, and she could barely hold him. He twisted, and she felt his claws sink into her back as she staggered up the ramp and half stumbled, half hoisted him into the back of the flying machine.

"DRIVE!" she yelled, banging her fist on the back of the cabin. "DRIVE, FRED! DRIVE!"

Fred must have heard her, for the flying machine made a sudden, deep gravelly sound and lurched forward. Maggie started to crank up the ramp. It was still hanging half open when there was a second deep gravelly sound followed by a loud pop. The engine cut out. They stopped, halfway up the hill, and slowly began rolling backward.

# Chapter 46

Rumpus gripped the floor of the strange vehicle to stop himself from sliding about. His claws made deep scratch marks in the patchwork of wood and metal. The girl was with him and that was reassuring, but everything else was the very opposite of reassuring. The vehicle kept jolting and jerking; the pops and bangs of the engine were noisy and alarming.

Abruptly, everything stopped.

All he could hear was the noise of the wagon wheels softly rolling backward. The ramp was only halfway up. The girl looked nervous but did not stop turning a large silver handle. A moment later, he heard footsteps, heavy thuds, and caught a whiff of stale nicotine. He backed himself as far into a corner as he could.

Suddenly a pair of hands gripped hold of the half-raised ramp. The men started shouting and yelling.

"Ned, give me a leg up! Now!"

"It's rolling backward! I can't!"

Rumpus heard groans and grunts as the man with

a thick beard and small eyes reared his head and shoulders over the rim of the half-raised ramp.

The girl dropped the crank and banged her fist hard on the wall.

"DRIVE! DRIVE, FRED, DRIVE!"

"You're not gonna get away with this, you little witch. That cat don't belong to you!" The man was still trying to pull himself in. He was almost inside.

PUFF-CLANK-POP-BANG!

The vehicle gave a sharp, almighty jerk forward and the engine roared back to life. They were moving again. Straining up the hill. Rumpus extended his claws, digging deeper into the floor panel. He hissed and let out a low growl. The noise and clouds of smoke were overwhelming. Somehow the man with the beard was still hanging on, shouting and shouting.

*Clink.* Rumpus turned and watched as the handle the girl had been turning one way began to spin in the opposite direction. Suddenly the ramp fell down, shuddering and jolting as the vehicle slowly gathered speed. With a final angry cry, the man who had been hanging on let go and tumbled backward down the hill. There were shouts and yells and a loud clattering as the tip of the ramp bounced and scraped along the lane.

The girl worked furiously on the crank, trying to get it back up. Rumpus felt sick. He kept sliding about. He turned around and around but couldn't find a way to lie down. They kept moving, bumping and clattering, the motion uneven and wobbly and quite fast now that they were up and over the hill.

The sharp left turn came unexpectedly as the vehicle swerved through a gate. The swinging sensation was too much for Rumpus. He felt his stomach contract, closed his eyes, and threw up.

# Chapter 47

Maggie clamped one hand over her mouth and gagged. Rumpus was being sick and the smell of it combined with the jolt and swing of the flying machine filled her to the brim with nausea. The journey had not lasted more than twenty minutes, but it felt like forever. She scrambled to one side and tried to breathe in the cold, fresh air, anything to relieve the smell.

They pulled into the cottage driveway just as dawn was breaking. Fred unwound the ramp, and Maggie caught a glimpse of Wildoak on the horizon, lit from behind by the glimmer of a rising sun. She felt a sudden wave of exhaustion.

"He's beautiful," whispered Fred, seeing Rumpus for the first time. His voice was laced with awe. Then he turned to Maggie. "You did it," he said. "You got him out."

"We did it, Fred," she said. "I couldn't have done this without you."

Fred smiled and helped her jump down. For a

moment, she looked back toward the gate. "Do you think, will those men f-f-f-f-find us?" she said.

"No," said Fred. "Once the old girl got going, we were much too quick for them." He patted the side of his cockpit. "But let's get Rumpus into his new pen and make sure everything is locked up safely," he added.

Maggie felt so tired and queasy, she could hardly find the energy to coax Rumpus into the new pen.

"Here," she whispered. "You're safe here." Reluctantly, he followed her.

"Come on, then, Maggie. Let's get you inside and up to bed. I think we could both use some sleep before we face tomorrow. I mean the rest of today," said Fred, glancing at the pale sky.

"Let me stay here, j-just a little while," Maggie said, looking across at Rumpus. "I don't want to leave him, not yet." She wasn't entirely sure that Brae Thatcher wasn't somehow hiding in the dark.

Fred opened his mouth and then closed it again. "All right," he said. "But I'm getting you some blankets." Rumpus slumped down in the far corner of the pen, his tail flicking restlessly from side to side. Maggie edged a little closer and lay down beside him. "I'm here," she said. "They can't get you now . . ." Her voice trailed off, and she felt her eyelids drop. She could not remember ever feeling so tired or so relieved.

Maggie woke a few hours later to the sound of a car pulling into the driveway. She rubbed her eyes, blinking in the crisp, cold sunlight, and shivered. Rumpus was still lying beside her, half-asleep. They lay in a tight curl, side by side on the ground, a thick wool blanket wrapped around her shoulders. Her head ached, and she felt groggy. She couldn't tell what time it was. And there was a terrible smell. She looked down at her corduroys. They were covered in sick. Then everything came flooding back: the rescue, Brae Thatcher, the ride home. She pictured Thatcher's angry face and winced, half expecting him to come knocking on Fred's door at any moment.

She rubbed her eyes again.

A car door banged.

She could hear voices now, familiar voices, a man and a woman. Maggie sat up. A flash of recognition and then the realization that *today* was Monday!

She leapt to her feet. Rumpus opened one eye but

didn't move. She left him inside the pen, locked the door, and raced around to the front of the house.

Vincent and Evelyn Stephens stood in the driveway as a taxi pulled out behind them. Maggie ran toward her mother and threw out her arms, breathless, burying her head inside the wool of her coat and the smell of her. She could not begin to unravel the array of emotions that seemed to engulf her.

"Maggie! Oh my goodness, I've missed you!" Mrs. Stephens hugged her in return, kissing the top of her head again and again. "My girl, oh, it's so good to see you!"

Maggie pulled back. She was smiling. And then frowning.

"I've missed you t-too, Mother," she said. Then, catching the look of surprise on her mother's face, she realized how disheveled she must have looked and how bad she must smell. Her cords were filthy, there were bits of leaves and sticks matted into her sweater, and her fingernails were rimmed with crescents of dirt.

"Margaret?" her father said, staring at her. "Goodness, what on earth has been going on here? Look at the state of you! The smell of you. Evelyn, look at the state of her!"

"Vince, just say hello," said Mrs. Stephens quietly. "What could you possibly have been doing?"

Maggie looked up at her father. "H-h-h-h-hello, F-F—F— —Father," she said. She could see the immediate disappointment in his gaze. She wasn't sure whether to try and hug him or not; his suit seemed so clean.

At that moment, Fred came out of the house, and while he looked tired, he was at least wearing fresh clothes. His footsteps ground into the gravel. The silence was thick and uncomfortable. Maggie felt jittery and fluttery, as if somebody had filled her stomach with a cloud of flies. Her eyes skipped between the three adults. Then Fred put out his hand.

"Vincent," he said. "Thank you for making the journey down. It has been"—he paused—"an eventful night. We've got a lot to talk about."

Mr. Stephens shook his hand in return but did not say anything. Maggie could tell from the set of his mouth that he was angry. Fred then turned toward her mother and hugged her for a long time.

"Hello, Dad," she whispered.

Mr. Stephens cleared his throat, breaking up their embrace. Then he leaned down to pick up one of the cases.

"Come along, then. And, Margaret, please, get yourself cleaned up," he added tersely, following Fred inside.

"Wait, Maggie," said Mrs. Stephens. She took off her gloves and dipped one hand into her coat pocket. "There's somebody else who wants to see you."

"Wellington!" Maggie felt a lump rise in the back of her throat. She scooped him into the palm of her hand and held him up to her cheek. "Oh, I've missed you," she whispered. "I've missed you so much. You'll have to meet Rumpus, but he won't hurt you. Well . . . we'll just have to be a bit careful." She turned to her mother. "Th-th-th-ank you so mmmm-much for bringing him, Mother."

Mrs. Stephens smiled and stroked Maggie's hair. She pulled out a small twig. "I wanted to bring Flute too, and Charlotte, and all the roly-polies, but it was too much. Mrs. Viner from next door is house-sitting though, so don't worry, they'll all be there when we get back. Now then, perhaps you should have a bath so we can catch up properly."

"Mother, I've got s-s-s-s-o much to tell you," said Maggie as they walked inside.

"I can't wait to hear everything," said Mrs. Stephens.

But no sooner had they reached the door than there was a loud, angry shout from the driveway.

Startled, Maggie turned around to see a group of men and women marching around the corner of the gravel track. Her stomach dropped. There at the front was Brae Thatcher and the man he'd been with last night. He carried a long, thick rope in his hands. The crowd looked angry. People saw her and started shouting more. Some carried rakes, spades, and long sticks.

"What on earth is going on?" said Mrs. Stephens. "Maggie, inside quick. Call your grandfather."

But Fred was already on his way out, followed closely by a stern-faced Mr. Stephens. "Let me handle this. I'll explain in a minute, I promise," said Fred, brushing past.

Mrs. Stephens turned to Maggie, confused. "I don't know what this is all about, love, but stay inside, go on, quickly."

"No," said Maggie, hesitating. "I n-n-n-n-need to ssssss-sssee what's happening."

Maggie felt a firm grip on her shoulder. "You heard your mother," said Mr. Stephens. "Inside."

But Maggie pulled away, escaping her father's grip, and ran toward Fred. He had his arms up and was waving them in the air, trying to urge the crowd backward.

A barrage of questions and comments flew at him.

"We know it was you, Fred! Give 'im up!"

"Let Brae do his job!"

"Look at the sight of that girl."

"She's a disgrace."

"Give up the monster, Fred, and we'll leave you be, none of us want to be here."

"It's what we all agreed, Fred! Give 'im up!"

"THAT'S ENOUGH!" Fred shouted. "None of you have any right, any right whatsoever to come marching down here like an angry mob. This is my property! Now, Sergeant Nichols—"

THUD. THUD. THUD.

Fred was cut off by the banging of a silver-knobbed cane against the gravel. Lord Foy stepped in front of the crowd.

"We have every right, Dr. Tremayne," Foy said, his voice firm. "That creature is a threat to our community and needs to be disposed of. This village is no place for a wild leopard, whatever your harebrained thinking on the matter. Sergeant Nichols is here to ensure the creature is put down, once and for all."

Maggie felt the bones in her knees go soft. She had let Rumpus down once before, but not this time. Not now. She touched Fred's arm lightly. He stared at her. She held his gaze for a second, then he nodded.

"There's s-s-s-s-something I want to s-aaaaaaaa-ay," Maggie began. "Ten da-a-a-a-a-a-a-ys ago, I found a snow leopard c-c-c-____aaught in a gin trap." She lifted her gaze and looked directly into the faces of the crowd. There were so many people, all listening. Her heart thumped, beating hard against her small ribs, sucking in the air and punching it out again. For a moment, she felt hot, so hot, and all the faces blurred together.

Everyone grew quiet.

All that Maggie could hear was the sound of her heart beating.

Somebody coughed.

The silence dragged on.

Maggie closed her eyes. She pictured the look on Rumpus's face when he had first opened his eyes and seen her, his paw gripped by the trap. How frightened he had been.

"His name," she said, raising her voice, "is Rumpus. He is not a m-m-monst-t-ter. He can't tell us h-how he came here or why. But whatever the r——reason, what he needs is h-h-help f-f-finding the right home. Finding a way to b-be, just be, himself. To live.

"Fred and I will find a place that ca——-a——a—n look after him, properly. It will take a little wh—wh—while, but in the meantime, we have a strong p-p-pen for him here. He c-c-c-cannot get out. He will be safe until we und—-d—-d——derstand what to do next. And you w—-i——i-ll be safe too. All of you.

"You have to un–n–n–n–n–derstand. He is not a m-m-m-monster. He is a living being, with f—-feelings and needs . . . just like the res-s-s-t of us. So, st-t-t-t-t-top trying to hurt him. And let him be, just as he is."

Maggie swallowed hard. She had said what she wanted to say. She had stuttered all the way through, but she had said exactly what she wanted to say.

Fred put a hand on her arm and squeezed it gently.

Something inside Maggie's fierce and loving heart broke free of itself.

*She had said what she wanted to say.*

It felt good, so good. Like nothing she had ever felt

before. She tried to find the right word to describe how she was feeling. Was it relief? No, it was more than that. Stronger than that. Pride? Yes. She felt a lightness, as if she was floating now. She felt proud of herself. She could be understood. *She could be heard.*

"Perhaps she's got a point," said a tall woman at the back.

"No, she ain't," said Brae Thatcher, shouldering his way through to the front. "She's done nothing but cause trouble since she got here. Big trouble." He spat on the ground.

Maggie lifted her chin a little higher and held his gaze.

# Chapter 48

Rumpus pricked his ears. One ear faced forward and the other bent backward, so it partially faced in the opposite direction. He could hear the sound of human voices, a crowd, noisy, on the other side of the house. Then the sound of the girl's voice. He would recognize it anywhere. He got up and began to pace. The chicken wire bothered him. He couldn't understand why he was being kept away from her.

# Chapter 49

Brae stared at Maggie, his eyes squinting in the light. Maggie stared back.

"Come now, Brae. She's said her piece. If he's locked up already, that's all we really wanted," said an older man in a tattered brown cap.

"I want to see the cage," said somebody else from the back. "Make sure it's safe!"

"QUIET!" Lord Foy shouted. He pointed the tip of his cane at Maggie's face. Maggie did not step back. "Who on earth do you think you are?" he said. "How dare you come into this village and tell us what to do? You're nothing but a common criminal, breaking into Nigel's farm, upsetting all the animals, *stealing*. You and your mad grandfather don't have the wherewithal to look after yourselves, let alone a wild cat." He turned to Fred, swinging his cane sideways. "Hand over the animal immediately or consider yourself in disobedience of the law."

Fred stared at Foy. "I will do no such thing."

Then a lot of things happened all at once.

Foy jabbed Fred in the chest with his cane, Brae Thatcher lunged at Maggie, and the whole crowd swelled forward. Maggie felt herself being pushed down, stumbling and falling. Mr. Stephens forced himself into the mix and grabbed hold of Thatcher by the scruff of his jacket, Fred slapped Foy's cane away, and Mrs. Stephens tried desperately to reach Maggie.

A loud whistle pierced the air.

"Everybody CALM DOWN!" shouted Sergeant Nichols. "It's time for all of you to go home. Including you, sir," he added sharply, looking at Lord Foy. "This whole situation is getting out of hand. Young Margaret has made her case, and I will personally investigate the safety of this matter, *alone*. For now, ALL of you need to go home." He blew his whistle again and waved his truncheon in the air. "Home! Now!"

A handful of villagers reluctantly began to turn away, murmuring their disapproval. Maggie looked up to see her mother reaching for her. Gingerly, she got up. Then she saw Foy retrieve his stick and point it at Fred.

"I'm not through with you, Tremayne," he said. "Mark my words."

"You'll never be through with me," replied Fred.

"Because you and I will never see this world in the same way." Then he snatched Foy's cane out of his hands and threw it away like a spear. "Now get out of my driveway."

Maggie watched as Foy shook his fist in the air, then turned and limped away. She brushed off her knees and hands.

"Margaret?"

She turned. Her father's tie was out of place, and he had a look on his face that she had never seen before. His eyes seemed . . . softer.

"That was quite a speech you just gave," he said. He sounded almost shaky. "I think we had better go inside and get cleaned up." He touched a raw scrape on the side of his brow. "Then you can tell us what all of this is about."

Maggie nodded. She watched him head back into the cottage, his hands thrust into his pockets. She followed, her footsteps lighter, her heart braver than before.

A short while later, Maggie sat at the kitchen table, having changed her clothes and cleaned her face. She expected her parents back down at any moment. She tapped her fingers against the surface of the table. Fred was making a pot of tea and some cheese sandwiches. A fresh wave of tiredness washed over her and she felt scared. Scared of not being able to find a safe place for Rumpus. Sergeant Nichols had left for now, but he had made it clear Rumpus could not stay for long.

"F-Fred?" she said. "What are we going to do?"

Fred lifted the lid of the teapot and dropped in a handful of fresh teabags. He was quiet for a moment. "I'm not quite sure, Maggie. Not yet at least."

"What if Sergeant Nichols says we have to . . . p-p-p-p-put him dow——dow——" She couldn't finish the word.

Fred came over and sat next to her. He took her hands in his.

"There's a woman I used to know, a long time ago. Her name is Molly Burkitt. She volunteered at London Zoo throughout the war. She was an amazing person. I've already tried to reach her. Apparently, she's moved to Scotland and is running a wildlife sanctuary there. The keeper I spoke to has given me an address and suggested we write to her. He seemed to think they've already got a snow leopard, a female, about the same age as Rumpus." He paused. "I promise you, Maggie, we'll find a solution. Somehow."

Maggie looked at him. It seemed like a long shot, but she knew he meant what he said. She just didn't know if it was truly possible. Rumpus didn't belong in a zoo, but he didn't belong in the Cornish countryside either. Even if by some miracle they found a way to release him back into the wild somewhere in China or Mongolia or wherever the encyclopedia had said he was from, he was too domesticated. He would never be able to survive on his own. She thought of his face, the emotion, the instincts, all of the things she knew that were buried inside him, the things he would say if only he could.

"Fred?" she added. "My stutter is never g-g-going to go away, is it?"

He squeezed her hands. His grip was warm and tender.

"Look at what you just did. You were amazing this morning. Your stutter didn't stop you, did it? You said exactly what you wanted to say. What you needed to say."

"But it was so hard. It still m-m-m-m-made me so scared."

"I know, love. I know. But at the end of the day, all you really needed was a little more time."

She squeezed his hands in return.

"But I still d-d-d-d-on't like my v-voice," she whispered. "People l-l-l-laugh at me. They don't t-t-t-take me seriously. I don't *want* to t-t-t-ake longer than everybody else."

"Everybody has something about themselves they want to change, Maggie. Whether it's the way they look, the way they sound, where they're from, what they own or what they don't." He paused. "Some of us feel it more than others. But the truth is, and I believe this with all my heart, there's room in this beautiful, complicated world of ours for all of us. Just as we are. In fact, there is a need for it."

Maggie was trying not to cry. He was right.

The kettle began to rattle and whistle. Fred let go of her hands and got up. Maggie wiped her eyes.

A moment later, Mr. Stephens walked into the kitchen.

"Hello, Vincent, I'm making us a bite to eat," said Fred. "I just need more milk from the pantry. Is Evelyn coming down?"

Mr. Stephens nodded. "She'll be right down. Thank you, Fred."

Fred stepped out for a moment. Maggie glanced up. She did not know what to say to her father. She wanted to say everything and nothing, all at the same time.

"This morning, in front of all those people. You—" Mr. Stephens began to speak but then stopped. She wasn't sure, but he almost seemed afraid.

"It's all right," she whispered. And for a brief moment, she was able to see herself from his perspective, to understand that she was part of the disorder he could no longer bear, that she was something he thought needed fixing.

But for the first time in her life, she realized that he was wrong. Completely wrong.

# Chapter 50

Rumpus paced inside his pen. Men had come, one wearing a black uniform with silver buttons and a strangely shaped hat. They had rattled the door of the pen, pulled on the locks, shaken the fence posts. The man in black had smelled of sweat and fear.

But still the girl had not come back.

He kept pacing, up and down, restless for her return. So many unfamiliar noises and smells disturbed him. Where was she?

He stopped and lifted his nose in the air, searching for her. He turned his head toward the house and waited.

She would come.

# Chapter 51

Once they had finished talking through all of the extraordinary things that had happened, Maggie desperately wanted to get back to Rumpus. But they continued to sit around the table in the kitchen, still supposed to be having lunch even though the time was almost three o'clock in the afternoon and nobody had eaten a thing. She tapped her fingertips impatiently against the underside of the wood. A sudden and unexpected quiet settled over the group.

Mr. Stephens cleared his throat. "You know there's one more thing we need to discuss," he said, his voice taking on an edge. "And there's no point ignoring it any longer."

"Hang on," said Fred quickly, putting down his sandwich. "As you've just heard, it's been a tough twenty-four hours. So if this is about Maggie's stutter, then let's talk about it tomorrow and—"

"I'm grateful to you for having her," cut in Mr. Stephens, "but we agreed that if the air down here didn't improve things . . . she would go to Granville Place for proper treatments." He paused and took a sip of water.

Maggie stared at a crumb of cheese on her plate. A wave of nausea rose up from the soles of her feet and rolled through her stomach. It had all been too good to be true. Father coming down like this, listening and talking to Fred. Asking questions about Rumpus.

"But I was wrong."

She looked up.

"Listening to you speak today, Margaret, standing up for this leopard, for yourself, for your grandfather, in front of all those people." He stopped and swallowed hard. "You *are* doing better. Perhaps not in the way I had expected. But you are doing better. Much better."

Maggie stared at him. At his dark green sweater, crisp white shirt, his shoulders rigid and tight. "B-b—b-ut—I thought—" she began.

"Let me finish," he went on. "Your mother and I went to look at Granville Place. And I'm ashamed to say it was not what I had thought it would be. Not at all. Which is why"—he paused, smoothing out the side of his hair—"we broadened our search. There is another school, St. Anne's Primary, that might work. It's a little farther away, but I think with some changes, we might be able to manage it."

Maggie turned to her mother. She could not quite believe what she was hearing. Mrs. Stephens reached out across the kitchen table. She smiled at Maggie. "You're not going to Granville," she said. Maggie squeezed her hand. "I told you Father would come around."

"Vincent," said Fred quietly, "I'm so glad."

"Well," said Mr. Stephens. "I suspected it was the right decision in the end, and now I'm sure of it." He coughed and placed his knife and fork neatly on his plate. Maggie held his gaze for a moment. He blinked hard. "So"—he cleared his throat and looked away quickly—"where is this snow leopard, then?"

"I can take y-y-y-you now," said Maggie, jumping up. "He won't hurt you, I p-p-promise. Well, maybe just a little bit, but not on p-p-purpose. He's very . . . playful." She grinned.

"Let me just get my camera," said Mrs. Stephens, smiling too. "I'd like to take some photographs."

The afternoon light was already beginning to fade as the four of them walked outside together. Maggie led them to the back of the cottage and around to the pen, where Rumpus was pacing back and forth. As soon as he saw her, he leapt with excitement.

"Hello," she whispered, slipping her fingers through the wire. Rumpus rubbed his cheek up against her hands, pushing against the wire and chuffing with delight.

"How incredible," said Mrs. Stephens. "He's beautiful! What's he doing?"

"It's just his way of g-g-g-g-reeting me. It's a sort of mix between a sn-sn-sn-sneeze, a snort, a cheek rub, and a hu—-ug. All in one," she laughed as the cat continued to press his shoulder against the wire and chuff some more.

Maggie unlocked the pen door and went inside. Rumpus galloped over, knocking into her legs and almost pushing her sideways. "Hi!" she said. "Careful."

He seemed bigger suddenly, his paws not quite so clumsy, his shoulders a little broader. She reached out her hand to stroke him, but he hooked her arm sideways and quickly tried to pull her to the ground. His claw accidentally caught the inside of her arm and pulled a long scratch down the sleeve of her coat.

Her mother gasped.

"Are you sure it's safe?" said Mr. Stephens, raising a sharp eyebrow.

"Yes, F-Father," said Maggie, quickly trying to hide the mark. "He doesn't mean any harm, he really doesn't."

Her parents exchanged an uncomfortable look.

Rumpus rolled onto his back and kicked up his hind legs, baiting Maggie further, daring her to play with him.

"Maggie, do be careful," added Mrs. Stephens.

"Oh yes . . . It's ok-ay."

"It's okay. For now, at least," said Fred. "But not much longer."

Maggie rubbed the thick soft folds of fur behind Rumpus's ears. She knew he would never hurt her on purpose. But it was true, he didn't seem to know the power of his own strength.

They all stayed, watching as Rumpus tumbled and teased, and Maggie went along with it, cuffing him now and again. Mrs. Stephens took some photographs, and Maggie smiled. Soon enough the sun went down and dusk fell across the sky. Fred encouraged everyone to come back inside for a fresh cup of hot tea.

"I'll be in s-s-s-soon," said Maggie. She wanted a few minutes alone with Rumpus. He rolled onto his side and stretched out his legs. Maggie flopped down beside him. She thought about everything that had happened: how she had first found him, trapped, and then almost lost him. About the raid on the farm and everything since. She thought about the magnificent old oak, about the message she now carried within her, the feeling of being part of something vast and mysterious.

She looked over at the fading horizon, toward Wildoak. It *was* hard to be human, she thought. But it was also beautiful, so beautiful. She thought about Fred and of all the magical and wondrous things he had collected and saved over the years . . . the nests, the husks, the pressed flowers, the dried leaves, the cowries and the acorns. *Acorns.*

She lingered until it got dark and a handful of stars glimmered in the blue-black sky, until it was time. Maggie glanced over her shoulder, back at the cottage. She could see her parents silhouetted against the living room windows, lit with the light of Fred's glowing fire. Perhaps things would be different between them now. She hoped so.

Rumpus flicked his tail and looked at her. Maggie reached out to touch his thick silvery fur. Then she got down on her hands and knees, leaning forward so that her face was almost level with his.

"We will find a safe place for you," she said. "Where you can be yourself and not be afraid. It won't be easy. None of this will be easy." She felt a pain in her heart. She couldn't bear the idea of ever having to say goodbye to him. "But you're going to be okay," she whispered. "Yes. You're going to be okay."

He looked at her, just for a moment, his eyes soft and trusting. And it seemed to Maggie that he was saying the same thing, to her. But his words were not made of sounds or letters, formed in the brain or the throat, spoken with mouths and tongues. They were not those sorts of words. They didn't need to be. She understood.

*It won't be easy, but it's going to be okay.*

The wind stirred the branches of the trees around Fred's house. Maggie looked up. She marveled at the interconnectedness of the stars and the vast night sky, at the rising of the moon and the setting of the sun, at the slow spinning of this one, singular planet. And she thought of the warm, dark hollowing inside the old oak that had shielded Rumpus from so much. She turned to face of the brow of the hill beyond. The jagged silhouette of what remained of the forest was barely visible in the distance. She put her arms around Rumpus and held him.

"I will speak for the trees," she whispered. "And I will speak for you. I promise."

TODAY

THE ASPEN INSTITUTE,

COLORADO, USA

# Epilogue

An older woman stands beside a large podium. Her hair is white, cut short, and her smile is wide and welcoming. One of her front teeth is chipped. She unscrews a bottle of water and takes a sip. Her hands appear steady, but on the inside she is working hard. Public speaking is hard for her.

Projected onto a huge screen to her left is a black-and-white photograph of a young girl nose to nose with a snow leopard. The girl is laughing, and the leopard's ears are pricked forward. His large paws rest on the girl's narrow shoulders. If you didn't know any better, you might think he was smiling. Underneath the photograph is the following quote:

*The least I can do is speak out for those*
*who cannot speak for themselves.*

—DR. JANE GOODALL

The woman clears her throat and the room falls silent. Three hundred people are looking at her, waiting to hear what she has to say.

"Good afternoon," she begins. "My name is M__________M___________M-Margaret Stephens. I have a stutter. Please be p____ppp-patient. I need a little more ti---ime to speak."

She looks into the eyes of her audience. On the outside, she appears calm and confident. But inside she is still fighting. She goes on to tell a story—of a distinguished international career devoted to nature conservation and of something bigger.

It begins with a walk in the woods and a snow leopard caught in a trap. She clicks through a series of slides, talking through each one. It is an extraordinary tale and the audience listens intently. In time, she comes to the end.

"R-Rumpus survived," she says. "Even though his life was not, c-could never have been, as it should have been, he was well cared for. And I was a-a-able to v-v-visit him fairly often at a wildlife sanctuary in Sc______Sc-c-cotland. He was content there, joining ano----oth-other snow leopard named Rosie. The keepers suspected the-e-e-e-e-y were related in some way. It's a special p__place and they have become leaders in education and c_c-c-c-c-c-________conservation efforts ever since."

She pauses and pulls up a picture of a huge, lightning-blasted oak tree in the middle of a forest clearing. "Unfortunately, the old oak did not fare so well. By the su-u-u-u-ummer of 1963, Wildoak Forest had been fully cleared. Today, there is no trace of it."

The next picture shows a large shopping mall.

The woman turns back to the audience, but as she does so, she pulls from her pocket a small brown acorn.

"However, Lord Foy did not get the last word. This acorn belonged to my grandfather. We managed to save many more from the branches of the old oak before it was cut down. He went on to lead reforestation efforts in Cornwall that resulted in thou–s–s–s–s_sands of new trees being p–p–p–p-planted before he died. Those trees are now taller than this b-b-b-b________building."

She shows a picture of a young forest, light slanting through the branches.

The woman appears small on such a large stage, but there is something vital about the way she commands the room. "Wildoak is where I first understood the fragility and interc-c-connectedness of all things. And it changed my life. It was there I came to understand that everything speaks . . . the birds, the insects, the animals, even the trees . . . all things speak. Just not the same language."

She clicks again, bringing up the final image of her presentation: planet Earth, luminous in shades of green, blue, brown, and white, bright as the stars it sits among.

"There is more to this world than we know. More to understanding one another than language made of words and sentences, letters or sounds formed by human m---mouths or in h-h-uman hands."

She smiles. Then she points to the screen.

"Th-this is the first p-------picture ever taken of planet Earth, by the c-crew of the Apollo 17 spaceflight in 1972, less than ten years after Wildoak was cleared.

She turns to look at the audience and slows her speech intentionally. "This b-beautiful, c-c-complex world is the only one we have. My grandfather taught me it is up to each of us to do what we c-can in our own small ways to protect it. Our actions count. Our voices m-m-m-matter. We must use them."

The people in the audience begin to clap, louder and

louder, until one by one, they rise from their seats in a standing ovation. From the podium, the woman bows her head. She has said what she wanted to say. There is still a great deal of work to do. She understands it won't be easy, but she is hopeful. She knows there is power in her words.

# Author's Note

## ON TREES AND REFORESTATION EFFORTS ALL OVER THE WORLD

Some years ago, I discovered the work of Suzanne Simard, a professor of forest ecology at the University of British Columbia, and later read *The Hidden Life of Trees* by Peter Wohlleben. I learned about the ways in which trees "talk" to one another through a delicate system of roots and fungi, and how forests function in similar ways to human communities. As somebody who grew up (mostly barefoot) in the English countryside, I was fascinated and delighted by this.

As is well documented and understood, conservation and reforestation efforts will play a critical role if humans are to counter the effects of climate change and preserve precious natural habitats all over the world. *We really are all connected.* Dr. Jane Goodall often talks about the impact each of us can make, every single day, in our own small ways. It may seem like the choices we make as individuals are too small to matter, but that's not the case. When lots of people make small changes, big things happen.

If you're a young person reading this and would like to take action right away or start your own project, check out Roots and Shoots, the youth action program of The Jane Goodall Institute. The program's website is full of inspiring stories and hands-on advice as to how you can get involved immediately, using your own voice to bring about change in your local community. It's also a great resource for adults and educators who might want to support young people in their efforts to build a better world: www.rootsandshoots.org

There are many organizations in lots of different countries that are working hard on reforestation in particular. Here are just a few that are worth learning more about:

One Tree Planted: www.onetreeplanted.org
The Nature Conservancy: www.nature.org
Conservation International: www.conservation.org
Eden Reforestation Projects: https://edenprojects.org
Andes Amazon Fund: www.andesamazonfund.org

## ON THE SALE OF BIG CATS AND CONSERVATION EFFORTS TODAY

It is true that the Pet Kingdom at Harrods, a famous London department store, used to sell "exotic" pets such as baby elephants, jaguars, leopards, and alligators. A few years ago, I came across an article about a lion cub that had been bought there in 1969 by two young backpackers. They named him Christian and brought him to their home on the King's Road. It was not long before the situation became impossible, and the two young men began their long and challenging efforts to release him into the wild. Eventually, they succeeded and he was rehabilitated in Kenya by conservationist George Adamson. Christian's story was a happy one, although sadly it was not representative of what happened to most of the big cats sold at the time. In 1976 the British government passed the Endangered Species (Import and Export) Act that finally put an end to any kind of legal exotic pet trade, and the Pet Kingdom turned to selling domestic animals such as cats, dogs, and rabbits. It stayed open until 2014.

I was researching Christian the lion and thinking about this story when a dear friend sent me a recording of Dr. Alan Rabinowitz, the renowned zoologist and conservationist, speaking at a Moth Radio Hour event in New York City. He was talking about his experiences as a child, how he had stuttered when talking to humans but not to animals, and how much comfort he had found in being close to his beloved pets. He recalled visiting the Bronx Zoo and seeing a jaguar, locked inside a bare room. In that moment, Alan decided that if he could, he would one day speak up for big cats in a way that they couldn't speak for themselves. And that is exactly what he did. He grew up to become a leading conservationist for the Wildlife Conservation Society, and then for Panthera, the wild cat conservation organization that he co-founded in 2006. Dr. Rabinowitz passed away in 2018, but his passionate mission and essential work continues all over the world.

Panthera is an inspirational organization that works to ensure a future for wild cats and the vast landscapes on which they depend. This is such an important mission if certain species are to be prevented from going extinct. To learn more about Panthera and how you can help, please visit www.panthera.org.

The Snow Leopard Trust is another organization that does fantastic conservation work, in this case specifically for snow leopards. Its aim is to protect the cat in partnership with the local communities that share its habitat and to understand more about this beautiful creature. Please visit www.snowleopard.org for more information.

It is also possible to symbolically adopt a snow leopard through the World Wildlife Fund species adoption program. Please visit www.gifts.worldwildlife.org to learn how.

## ON STUTTERING AND WHERE WE ARE TODAY

Fortunately, our understanding of what it means to stutter has come a long way since Maggie was a child in the 1960s. (In the UK, the word "stammer" is more commonly used than the American "stutter," but they both refer to the same thing.) Today, there are a range of caring and dynamic organizations that provide a huge amount of support, encouragement, and opportunity for young people who stutter. If you are a young person who stutters or you have a friend or family member who does and would like to find out more, please check out the Resources section at the end of this note for detailed information on where and how to research further.

### WHAT STUTTERING IS AND WHAT IT ISN'T

Stuttering is a communication difference that can cause interruptions in a person's speech that they can't always control. It is caused by differences in the way the brain processes speech, but is not reflective of differences in intelligence or mental health. Stuttering is also extremely unpredictable and varies from one individual to the next. It can change from day to day or seem to disappear at times. Although there have been decades of research into how and why the brain processes speech differently in some individuals, the specific causes remain unclear. But we do know that it is *not* an emotional condition, meaning it is not, as it is often misunderstood or stereotyped, an indication of something like nervousness. Some people stutter *more* when they are relaxed and around people they are close to, some less; for some it makes no difference whatsoever who they are addressing. There may be similarities in certain repetitions, elongations of sounds or blocks, but there may not. Some people who stutter, like Maggie, might speak fluently to animals but not to people, some might sing without stuttering, others not. There are no set "rules" for how a person stutters; each individual has their own unique voice, however it may sound. It is also important to know that people who stutter are more than capable of being effective communicators—sometimes listeners will pay closer attention to a person who stutters.

If you are not a person who stutters, when you meet a person who does: Listen. Be patient. That's all.

## RESOURCES FOR YOUNG PEOPLE WHO STUTTER

1. **The Stuttering Association for the Young (SAY)** www.say.org
   SAY offers comprehensive and innovative programs in the US that address the physical, social, and emotional impacts of stuttering. Through summer camp (www.campsay.org), regional day camps, speech therapy, and creative arts programming, SAY builds a community of acceptance, friendship, and encouragement where young people who stutter can develop the confidence and communication skills they need to thrive.

2. **FRIENDS: The National Association of Young People Who Stutter** www.friendswhostutter.org
   FRIENDS provides support and education to young people who stutter, their families, and professionals, through annual conferences, online programming, one-day workshops, and outreach. Its vision is to help build a world in which all young people who stutter feel empowered to communicate whenever, wherever, and however they want to.

3. **The Stuttering Foundation** www.stutteringhelp.org
   The Stuttering Foundation provides free online resources, services, and support to those who stutter and their families, as well as assistance for research into the causes of stuttering. It also offers training programs on stuttering for professionals.

4. **National Stuttering Association (NSA)** www.westutter.org
   The NSA is dedicated to bringing hope and empowerment to children and adults who stutter, their families, and professionals, through support, education, advocacy, and research.

5. **American Institute for Stuttering (AIS)**
   www.stutteringtreatment.org
   AIS provides universally affordable, state-of-the-art speech therapy to people of all ages who stutter, guidance to their families, and much-needed clinical training to speech professionals wishing to gain expertise in stuttering. Its mission extends to advancing public and scholarly understanding of this often-misunderstood disorder.

These are just a few of the many organizations that are available to young people who stutter, as well as their families and friends. If you are a young person who stutters, or you are friends with somebody who does and you're looking for a supportive community, these are all great places to reach out to. Wherever you are on your journey, know that you are not alone, and they want to hear from you.

# Acknowledgments

It is true that every book takes a village and there are many names that ought to be on the cover of this one. To my editor, Tracy Mack, thank you for seeing something true and tender in this story and for reading with such extraordinary care and compassion. To the whole team at Scholastic and Diana Sudyka for her beautiful art. Thanks to each of you. I'm in awe of what it takes to bring a book into this world.

To Elizabeth, thank you for your strong and steady guidance. I will always be more grateful to you than I can say. Casey, you read every draft with your capacious heart and poet's eye. I could not do this without you. Leah, thank you for your luminous friendship, warmth, and wisdom. Wendy, you've kept me going from the beginning, first class, first line. This is as much your book as mine. Thanks to you and Warren for holding me steady, always. And dear Patti, I thank you for the seriousness with which you take this task of writing for children. From the heart, as you always say. I will carry your soulful wisdom always.

To my friends and extended family members who stutter today and who stuttered when you were younger. Thank you for being you, exactly as you are. I will always be inspired by you. My heartfelt thanks goes especially to the following: Sara MacIntyre, thank you for your patience and kindness in answering so many of my questions early on and encouraging me to at least try to do this. I am deeply grateful to you. To Megan Whalen and to Molly Starkey for your thoughtful and considered feedback on early drafts. Your input was invaluable and helped shape this book in critical ways. Thank you. And to Taro Alexander. Thank you for your honesty, patience, expertise, and compassion in reading multiple versions, for helping to make this book the best it could be and for supporting this work of fostering empathy and understanding through story.

To Sarah Dugger, zoologist and big cat whisperer. Thank you for your thoughtful feedback on snow leopard behavior and for giving me the opportunity to go behind the scenes and interact with such extraordinary beings.

To Stacy, without whom none of these threads would have ever come together. Thank you for reading so many versions over the years, for all your expertise and feedback, for your belief in this book and what lies at the heart of it.

To my family, my heart. My brother, Rob, your endless encouragement and faith have kept me going through the deepest of doubts. You light the way whenever I feel lost. To Andrew, who has his hand at my back and always has, since I was six years old and running my heart out, last. I am inspired by everything that both of you do, and all that you are. To Lindsay, my sister, my rock. I couldn't get through without you. To dearest Laura, your kind and gentle heart knows no boundaries. Thank you for always being there for me. (And for your truly unbeatable cake.)

To Mum and Dad, I can never thank you enough for making so much of my life possible in the most blessed of ways. For a childhood full of books, conkers, dens, cats, dogs, and the freedom to make as many mud pies as I wanted. Thank you for always supporting me and for fostering in each of us a deep love of the countryside. Thank you for all of it.

And to my beloved nephews and nieces, Kit, Clara, Maya and dear Madeline, because in all of you I see a brighter and more compassionate future for this planet. To Unkie, who dared me to dream. To all of my Italian and American families, Marina, Armyne, Frank, Momo, Kearney, Kate, Ben, and Molly, and the best of outlaws, John, Dan, Sarah, and George for cheering me on no matter what. I am truly blessed to have each of you in my life.

To Papa, thank you for your steady smile and for teaching me about the stars. I will always feel your heartfelt encouragement at my side. We will miss and love you always.

And to my children, Una and Will. You have in your own ways taught me more about what matters most in this world than I could ever have imagined. You are my inspiration, my light. For the record, I love you mostest.

I am honestly not sure who reads these end pages, let alone all the way to the very, very end, but if you are still reading, forgive me for sharing a final note of gratitude. It is the last, but it is the most meaningful to me. A long time ago I met a young American with a huge and generous smile who listened more than he talked. JCH, I thank you the most. Thank you for the days, for each and every one.